Write Michigan 2022 Anthology

Chapbook Press

Chapbook Press
Schuler Books
2660 28th Street SE
Grand Rapids, MI 49512
616.942.7330
www.schulerbooks.com

ISBN 9781957169033

Sofia Armas	**Payton Kalsbeek**
Amelia Bogertman	**Elijah Kuiper**
Dev Buysse	**Brenna LaForge**
Kevina Clear	**Meredith Mead**
Ellie Einfeld	**Will Miedema**
Sylvia Fisher	**Lily Orange**
Julie Foust	**Miguel Rafah Reagan**
Paige Harry	**Sevie Roddy**
Meghan Hemmer	**Chris Sorenson**
Colette Horvath	**Sofia Toboy**
Loretta Jahncke	**Amelia Veltman**
Adi Jain	**K.S. Walker**

Cover art ©2021 Adolfo Valle | adolfovallestudios.com

Printed in the United States by Chapbook Press.

Table of Contents

Foreword

By Stephen Mack Jones

My father lived a hard life.

By the age of twelve, he was driving a coal delivery truck (how most homes were heated in the 1930s and '40s) to contribute money to the small house he shared with his three brothers, sister and parents. All of my father's family worked—cleaning houses, factory and janitorial—in order to keep the lights on, the coal-burning furnace stoked in winter and at least two meals a day at their small home on Hammond Street in Lansing, Michigan. He left school in the 10th grade so he could work longer, harder for his family. And when war came to the world in 1940, my father joined the U.S. Army where he faced bitter, hate-hardened adversaries at Fort Benning, Georgia. A place where the local population promised violence to any Negro seen wearing any uniform of the U.S. Armed Forces. I have a photo of my father wearing his Army dress uniform; he's laughing. He's laughing as if those threats meant nothing. He's laughing as if the bad juju of Southern white people meant little to him. After all—he'd driven a truck and delivered tons of coal when he was twelve. That takes any childhood fear of boogey-men and monsters right out of you.

But for all of his hard, callous-hand-and-bloody-knuckled life, he had two true and steadfast companions: My mother and books.

Before a long, twelve-hour shift at the local Oldsmobile automobile factory in Lansing, he had a book in his hands. My mother at times had to remind him to put whatever book he was reading down long enough to eat. Begrudgingly, he would eat if only to store energy to get through his day or night shift. And he would return home, exhausted, smelling like hot steel. He would again eat, if only to renew his energy for at least an hour's worth of reading before bed.

What did this high school drop-out read?

Treasure Island and Pilgrim's Progress.

Principles of Mechanical Engineering and the poetry of Robert Frost and Langston Hughes.

Books on financial investment strategies and James Baldwin novels.

And Shakespeare.

Always the plays of William Shakespeare.

I was five+ years old when my father came home—smelling like the hot grinding gears of a giant machine—grabbed me up and pushed me into the front passenger seat of our rusting used car.

"You're old enough to have one now," he said as we drove.

One of what? I wondered.

He seemed uncharacteristically happy for someone who'd just finished a ten-hour blue-collar factory job, so I didn't ask. I wanted him to be happy. I always wanted him to be happy. If only for a few minutes in a day. One week out of a year.

We parked in front of the new Lansing Public Library and he told me it was time for me to have my own library card. Still seated in the car and staring up at the new, modern library building, he told me the world he grew up in had been small and tough and short-sighted. But books— reading—had taken him to the pyramids of Egypt and the furthest reaches of outer space. Books had transported him to the long disappeared Jewish villages of Russia to the distant futures of Isaac Asimov and Ray Bradbury. Books had given him hope where once there was none, and promise where there was little.

"I didn't have much of a chance to be a kid and get an education," he said as we got out of our car and walked into this shiny new building across the street from green city space called Reuter Park. "I want to make sure you and your brother have both. And besides me and your mom, your education starts right here."

Still wearing his dark blue, sweat-stained work clothes, my father stood me in front of the library's long, sleek circulation desk. A woman smiled at us and said, "May I help you?"

My father gave me a slight nudge and said, "Tell the nice lady why you're here?"

Hesitantly and in a small voice, I said, "I'd like to get a library card." My father nudged me again, prompting me to add, "Please."

The librarian's eyes widened as did her smile. She spoke directly to me instead of my father, as if I were the most important person she'd met—at least on that particular late spring day.

"Yessir," she said brightly. "Let's get you your very own library card, shall we? What do you like to read?"

"Mostly books about space."

"Oh," she said. "We have a lot of books about space! Fiction and non-fiction. They say in several years we'll be able to fly people to the moon—"

"And Mars!" I added.

She gave a gentle laugh. "Yes. And Mars."

After five minutes, I had my very first library card which felt like I'd been handed the keys to a fantastic kingdom. An empire that answered unquestioningly to my commands. A place where I, at five-years of age, could ask any librarian any question and they were duty-bound to answer. Adults who answered to me in my quest for books about other worlds, other people, customs and creatures.

Soon after receiving my first library card and making the newly minted library my second home, I realized something that would forever change me: For as much as I enjoyed reading stories others had written, there was a growing need in me to tell stories that were forming in me. Stories that would guide me to a better understanding of myself and the world I lived in. Stories that would help others understand themselves and the world they lived in. And thus, the journey to find my own storytelling voice began, aided by my mother, father and older brother. And, of course, my second beloved family—the librarians at the Lansing Public Library. Those women and men who listened to the small voice of a curious child without judgement or reservation. The ones who challenged me to widen my view of storytelling horizons and to think longer and deeper about my own reading needs. The people I followed with implicit trust down book-crowded corridors and narrow, book shelf-lined hallways until just the right book appeared as if long awaiting my arrival.

Over the years, I've visited a number of libraries in America and Europe. Every one of them feels like home. Every one of them welcomes me to the fascinating wonders and tantalizing secrets they offer. Every one of them kept alive and vibrant with librarians ready, willing and able to guide me to books that have been awaiting my arrival.

As to reading as an exercise to find my own unique writing voice?

Well, to be quite honest, every book I've ever read has told me the same thing which is, "We may enjoy each other's company, but I most certainly am not your voice, Steve. You are your own voice. All you have to do is trust yourself to speak your truth openly, honestly and without regrets or worries."

And though I'm sure I will be haunted tonight by the clanking chains of Ghosts of Grammar Teachers Past, you will most likely not find your voice in the spiraling depths of split-infinitives, dangling participles, or the correct placement of the Oxford comma. You will find your voice where it's always been: in your heart, your mind and soul. It is in your experiences, your small adventures and large questions. It is your triumphs and, most importantly, your failures.

Your voice is alive.

Right now.

And it's waiting to be heard . . .

About the Author

Stephen Mack Jones is a published poet, an award-winning playwright, and a recipient of the prestigious Kresge Arts in Detroit Literary Fellowship. He was born in Lansing, Michigan, and currently lives in Farmington Hills, outside of Detroit. He worked in advertising and marketing communications for a number of years before turning to fiction. His novels include *August Snow* and *Lives Laid Away*. His most recent book *Dead of Winter* was selected as a 2022 Michigan Notable Book.

Adult Judges' Choice Winner

Serendipitous
Brenna LaForge

"Antique hand grenades are not approved desk décor, Poppy."

I glanced up from my desk, smirking at Cal as he strolled into the archive, a disposable coffee cup in each hand. I set down the small brush I was holding and peeled off my white gloves.

"Even if it's defunct?" I questioned, picking up the small, ridged object that was sitting a foot away by my desk lamp. "At least, I think it is."

Cal's eyes went wide for a moment before I broke the tension with a chuckle. His shoulders slumped with relief. I set the bomb back in its spot, where it waited for a turn with my brush.

"Not funny." he snipped, even though his mouth curled at the corner. He set one of the cups down in front of me. "Hot chocolate, as always."

I picked it up, eyeing the delicate scroll sitting inches from where he'd placed it. I stopped myself from thinking about what would happen if any of my drink had spilled on it.

"Thanks. Wish I liked coffee; I could really use the caffeine."

He raised an eyebrow and surveyed me. "Have you been here all night?" I gave a noncommittal shrug. "I like when the building is quiet."

He rolled his eyes. "You work alone on the third floor of the museum. In a secure wing that requires a special-issued badge. I mean, no one can even call your desk phone without a special passcode. No one has as much quiet as you do."

I sipped at my drink, my patience melting away with every word he spoke. "Well, thanks again for my hot chocolate." I turned my back to him and set the cup down on the other desk I used for formal paperwork and database research. I tapped the space bar a couple times and the computer buzzed to life, the login page appearing. I glanced over my shoulder, giving a not-so- subtle hint that I was done with our conversation and was waiting for him to leave so I could put in my password.

I heard him sigh. "Don't forget the world outside, Poppy. Each of these items has a story to tell, and I know you'll do them justice. But what about your story? You still have time to write it."

My jaw twitched as I listened to him leave.

What gives him the right to tell me how to live my life? I'm only 23 years old, and I've got plenty of time to "write my story".

I was happy to sit at my quiet desk and discover the secrets of the artifacts. Holding something in my gloved hands that someone held decades (or even centuries) ago always felt so grounding. My work held meaning, and therefore my life held meaning. *Right?*

I dove right back into my work, muttering to myself for the next twenty minutes about the importance of preserving history.

A short while later, I was looking through a small metal tin that held several black and white photographs. I shuffled through them, making an inventory of each one and any notations on the back. Most of them were snapshots of a group of teens participating in various summer activities, dated 1941. They seemed to be your average activities, like riding bikes, having a malt at the local malt shop, and swimming in a suspicious-looking pond. But as I shuffled the photo of a young woman jumping off a dock to the back of the pile, my heart skipped a beat.

The very next photo was by all means just as average as the others, but something about it suddenly caused me a great deal of grief.

Déjà vu is a French expression, meaning "already seen". Oftentimes people feel as if they have experienced or dreamed of something before, but science is still attempting to figure out what in our brains causes it. But what I was feeling didn't come from my brain; it came from my heart. And in my heart, I knew that I had seen one of these men before.

The photo appeared to be two young men, roughly eighteen to twenty years old. They were wearing leather bomber jackets, each with an arm around the other's shoulders. They faced the camera, genuine laughing smiles on their faces.

The man on the left looked about six feet tall, with dark blonde hair. He was pleasant, but he wasn't the one I recognized. The young man beside him was the one who had me feeling perplexed.

He was a couple inches shorter than his friend, with dark hair and a slightly crooked smile. His teeth were straight and white, and his eyes were light-colored – most likely blue. He had a strong jaw, and a slightly cleft chin. He was dashing.

But where did I know him from? It didn't seem possible. I mean, the photos were all roughly from the same time – 1940-1941. My parents hadn't even been born yet, so there was no way that I had met him. But had I seen him somewhere, I was sure of it.

I dropped the photos back into the tin and closed it. I pulled off my gloves and pinched the bridge of my nose. *I must be suffering from sleep deprivation.*

Admitting defeat, I rose from my desk and gathered my belongings. I was going to call a cab to take me home because my brain obviously wasn't functioning at full capacity.

I shrugged on my coat and reached for my bag when I saw a tiny spark erupt from the back of my desk phone. The phone was an old rotary model that I'd picked up at an antique store last year. The IT guys were not excited about hooking it up for me, but after enough convincing, they'd connected it with a warning about old wiring. Their warnings suddenly had a bit more merit.

Just as I reached out to unplug it from the wall, the phone rang. It was my password- protected desk phone, so it was either something urgent or Cal was calling to see if I was still at my desk. The phone was so ancient that it didn't have caller ID, so I couldn't be certain. I would have to risk injury just this once.

I picked up the heavy receiver and answered. "Hello?"

The other line crackled. "Margie?" A low, male voice called out. He sounded like he was far away, or I was listening to him speak from the other end of a long tube.

I narrowed my eyes. "No, this is Poppy in Archives. Who is this?" I glanced at the phone wire and plug, but everything was fine. No fire, at least.

"Poppyin R. Kives?" the male voice laughed. "Who stuck you with a name like that?"

"That's not my name." I snapped. "I'm Poppy. I work in the archives at the Beecher Museum. Who is this?"

"Archives? Gee, that operator must've connected me to the wrong number. I was looking for Margie King on 38th."

I blinked, unable to fathom how he was able to not only get my number correct but get past the four-digit passcode that I had put in to prevent unnecessary conversations, which I changed monthly.

"What's your name?" I asked. "You aren't in any trouble; I just need to know how you got this number."

He didn't even pause before he answered. "My name is Thomas. And I didn't get this number. That new broad working the switchboards said she was connecting me to Margie, and the next minute I get you."

Broad? Switchboards?

"Switchboards, huh?" I rolled my eyes. "Seriously, who uses a switchboard in this day and age?"

Thomas sounded a little less cordial. "Hey, now. We don't all have those new manual phones, ace. Some of us still got the Doris Jones' of the world working our switchboards."

Was this guy pranking me? Sure, prey on the history nut for loving the past. Ha ha.

"Okay, hot shot, who put you up to this? Was it Cal?" I glanced through the small window in the archives' door but didn't see anyone watching me. I looked up at the singular camera that guarded over the expensive items in their expensive acid-free boxes and glared with white-hot anger.

The young man on the other end sounded confused. "Cal? I don't know any Cals. Wait, is this some sort of war thing? Are they testing me before I enlist?" His voice was echoing a little and I stretched the receiver away from my ear.

War?

I was growing more and more confused by the second. Fueled by almost no sleep and the tiny slice of me that hoped it could be exactly what my irrational side was concocting, I quietly asked, "Thomas, I'm sorry, but could you tell me- what's the date again?"

"November 21, 1941, ma'am."

My heart dropped in my chest. A wave of nausea hit me like a brick wall. I could feel my chest tighten.

"Ma'am, are you alright?" I heard Thomas ask, his voice quiet and patient.

I swallowed hard, trying to calm down. "I'm sorry." I choked out. *How do you explain to someone that you're from eighty years in the future?*

"Don't be sorry, Poppy. I'd be happy to sit here with you for a minute if you need it."

What a sweet guy. I was having a near-breakdown and he was being a gentleman to a stranger.

"Thanks." I took a couple more breaths. I couldn't have him hanging up on me just yet.

There was so much I wanted to know. "Distract me. What are your plans for the day?"

"Well, my pal Louis and I were going to take Margie and Mary to the dance hall tonight. That's why I was calling her, to let her know that I'm gonna pick everyone up. It's our first date, actually." He sounded coy, almost bashful.

"First date, huh?" I smiled. "Where did you meet her?"

"School. I graduated last year, but she's still got a year left. I was going to the college a few towns over, but I decided to come home. I'm going to enlist."

"That's quite honorable." I grimaced at the thought of this kind boy in the brutality of war.

"Well, dad says that our joining the war is inevitable. I figure I better do what I can."

He had no idea how right his dad was. Within the next three weeks, the United States would indeed be joining the war. Soon, the draft would sweep millions of eligible young men into uniforms and off to battle. My heart ached thinking about all those who had been lost to the second World War.

"Thomas, if it isn't too much of an intrusion, what's your last name?"

"Collins, ma'am. Thomas Collins, though most people call me Tommy."

Déjà vu hit again. This time, it was much stronger, and it was accompanied by a shot of dread straight into me like adrenaline.

I knew where I'd seen his face before. And it was so much worse than I had imagined.

I had to choke back a gasp. "Tommy, can you hold on a moment? Please, don't hang up. *Promise me you won't hang up.*" I begged, my voice thick with desperation.

He was quiet for a moment, and then he said, "Yeah, sure."

I set the receiver down gently against my desk and leapt out of my chair. I shed my coat as I ran down the center aisle toward the row where I stored the newspapers.

The box of newspapers I'd finished inventorying last week was still on the floor at the very end of the row, waiting to be re-filed. The light brown box was short and wide, and about as inconspicuous as any of the others around it. But what sat inside was suddenly more important than anything else I'd ever touched.

I tore the lid off and began to sort through the papers, looking for the one dated November 22, 1941. Tomorrow's newspaper.

At last, I found it. I pulled it from the box with a satisfying swish and carried it back to my desk. I set the fragile paper down, not bothering to put on my white gloves. A silent tear slipped down my cheek as I re-read the front-page headline: Three teens dead, one injured in car crash.

"Three teens lost their lives and one is in critical condition after a car accident on Friday evening. The four teens were on their way to the dance hall that evening when the accident occurred. The victims include Miss Margaret Price, Mr. Louis Rossini, and Mr. Tommy Collins. The other passenger, Miss Mary Finley, remains in critical condition at St. Damian's Hospital. Authorities reported that poor weather and icy roads led to the car leaving the road and breaking through a guardrail. The car plummeted down more than 100 feet into an embankment, where it sat for several hours. Police were only contacted when none of the teens reported home by 10:00 that evening. They were discovered around 2:00 AM and the three fatalities were pronounced on the scene. Funeral services will be announced later."

Tommy was going to die on the way to the dance hall tonight.

I had a decision to make. I wasn't that big into science fiction, but I figured that coming right out and telling him how he was going to die was only going to cause more problems. But I couldn't let him go without a warning.

I lifted the receiver and put it up to my ear. "You still there, Tommy?" "Yes, ma'am."

"Listen, Tommy. I'm going to say something that's going to sound completely nuts, but I need you to be open-minded. Can you do that?"

Silence responded. My heart thundered in my chest. After a moment he said, "Yes, ma'am."

I nodded, sighing. "Look, I'm just going to come out with it. I don't know how, but somehow when Doris connected our call... something crazy happened. It's November 21st here too... but I'm in the year 2021."

More silence. "Tommy?"

"I'm here." He muttered. "But that's a hard one to accept, ma'am."

"I can't prove much, other than this." I glanced at the sports section of the page and listed off a couple scores. "Check those numbers in the morning. But first, please... don't go tonight."

"Excuse me?"

I winced. "I know you want to go. But something bad... is going to happen. You must trust me. Please, for me? Don't go. If not for me, then for Margie."

"Something bad's gonna happen to Margie?" his tone had gone from weary to ice cold.

"Yes."

"Well, I..."

A shrill voice interrupted. "Tommy, I need the line. Sorry, doll." Doris.

"Wait!" I called out. "Just another minute, please." "Sorry, Poppy." Tommy mumbled.

"No, you've gotta listen to me. Please!"

The line went dead. I began to sob as I hung up the phone.

It had only been five minutes, but it had felt like the longest five minutes of my life. A man's life held in the balance, a glimpse of the past direct from the source... it was a lot to take in.

I waited another ten minutes, staring at the phone. When it didn't ring, I finally unplugged it from the wall and gathered my belongings. I need a vacation.

As I headed through the main lobby, my heart was heavy. I'd done what

I could with the time I had. Perhaps if I'd had longer, I could have done a better job of convincing him not to go. I pulled on my beanie as I prepared to head outside into the frigid November air to hail a cab.

"Poppy?"

I glanced up to see a young man I'd never met before looking at me. He looked to be in his mid-twenties, with dark brown hair and light blue eyes.

"Uh, yes?" I replied.

The young man smiled, and his smile made me warm inside. It reminded me so much of the photo of Tommy. *It couldn't be...*

"I have something for you." He held out a small envelope, with my name scrawled in shaky lettering across the front.

I took the envelope from him and tore it open.

November 21, 2015

Dear Poppy,

I hope this letter finds you well.

When I had that serendipitous conversation with you, I thought you were a little crazy. But I figured that crazier things had happened. I called my friends and cancelled on them. And all those scores you gave me were exactly right. I knew you were the real deal. My guardian angel.

And so here I am... 93 years old. I never once thought I'd live this long, especially after surviving the war. But I've had a wonderful life. Margie and I did have our first date – and we had many more dances in the 61 years we were married. I'm surrounded by my children and grandchildren, and I'd like to think it's all because of you.

I can never thank you enough.

- Tommy Collins

I didn't realize I was crying until I saw a tear fall onto the letter. I looked up at the young man in front of me and smiled. "He survived."

"He lived to be 94 years old. His dying wish was for me to deliver this to you on this date at the Beecher Museum."

I tucked the letter safely into my bag. "Thank you."

The young man held out his hand. "My name is Lucas Collins." I grasped his hand with mine. "Poppy Meadows."

He grinned. "Who stuck you with a name like that?"

I laughed, feeling a confidence take over me that had been quiet for so long. "Join me for lunch and I'll tell you everything."

"I'd love that."

I suppose I'm finally writing my story after all, and this seems like just the beginning.

About the Author

Brenna LaForge is from Battle Creek, MI. She discovered her love of reading and writing very young, and still remembers spending hours typing away on her family's desktop computer. After years of working in libraries, archives, and museums, she received her Bachelor of Public History degree from Western Michigan University, turning her love of history and books into a career. When she's not at work in her local library or writing her next story, you can find her taking walks with her husband and daughter, eating movie theater popcorn, or watching her favorite YouTubers playing horror games. You can discover more from her on Wattpad, Inkitt, and Instagram as @brennaiswriting

Adult Judges' Choice Runner-Up
It's Beginning to Look a Lot Like Robots
Loretta Jahncke

It's December, the time of year when our thoughts turn to presents and parties, snowflakes and Santa, and, of course, robots. At least that's where my thoughts turn.

You see, I am what is known as a "creative person," which sounds great until you realize that means everyone wants you to make them something. So at Christmastime, when most people are waiting in line at the mall or staring at a computer screen hoping for free express shipping, I'm busy. Out-of-my-head-CRAZY busy, in fact.

Three years ago, I created a new Christmas cookie recipe. It required a little extra effort and a new definition of "genetically modified," but the cookies were fabulous. Everyone begged for the recipe, but I knew if I gave it out, I'd have the FDA on my case (again), so I just promised that I would make them again the next year.

And, I did. But, as I said, I'm a creative person and don't like to get in a rut. So, two years ago, in addition to my "secret recipe" cookie, I also gave everyone scarves, knitted out of a new space-age fiber. Thankfully, NASA dropped the industrial espionage charges when they found out I was using it for Christmas presents, instead of selling it to Google or the Russians. (I'm not sure why Google wanted it, but I don't blame the Russians. Those scarves would be awesome during a Moscow winter.)

But, the court order was pretty clear that I couldn't use it again, even if I did all of the production myself, until NASA's patent wears off. So I guess that's the last time for those scarves for a couple more decades. It's just as well, though. All of that knitting took forever, and since my cookie recipe is a little more labor-intensive than most recipes, I was pretty worn out by Christmas.

Last year, I learned my lesson and found ways to streamline the process. With a little automation and some slightly-more-radioactive materials, I shaved at least 2 months off the cookies. Not as much as I was hoping for, but enough to get my Christmas cards out on time. And, I tinkered around with some spare parts and managed a few remote-controlled toys for the nieces and nephews to play with. The remotes only lasted a few weeks until the Department of Defense (or is it Defense Department? They say it every time, I should remember by now) took the remotes in the last raid on the house. Honestly, you'd think they'd have more secure launch sequences by now. Good thing the Canadians are so forgiving.

Unfortunately, when the Defense Department came for the remotes, they also took my cookie-making supplies. Ive been experimenting with other recipes, but they're just not as good. Besides, Mark, the FBI guy that watches me, keeps intercepting my supplies.

"Confiscating contraband," he says. "Stifling my creativity," I say.

Now it's December again, and I have no secret-recipe cookies, nothing to knit, and my own personal Man-In-Black literally stealing my good ideas. (Mark says "Confiscating." Whatever.) That, my friends, is where the robots come in.

I've had them built and their AI programmed for months now, but I can't figure out what to do with them. We've talked about it, the robots and I , and nobody can come up with anything.

Oh, I shouldn't have call them, "the robots." They absolutely hate it! They are constantly calling Mark out on it. "We do have names, you know! How would you like it if we called you 'the humans?'"

Mary's the most sensitive to it. Once she overheard Mark and I talking about my Christmas dilemma.

"If you're so worried about Christmas, why not just give the robots as gifts? You and I both know how easy it would be for you to make more."

At the time, I was too outraged to notice his emphasis on that "you" and the touch of sarcasm in his voice. I only noticed later, when a tearful Mary played it back to me.

"How could you say that?! They're family - you don't just give away family!"

I'm glad I found the right words, for Mary's sake. She's always felt a little left out, since Nate and Joey have each other. I think maybe I should have made another girl for her to play with, but I don't know. It's such hard work taking care of them, ad I don't think I could handle another one right now. I've mentioned this to Mark before, but he just got a weird smile on his face and said, "Yeah, I can imagine it's tough being a single mom."

I don't understand why he was smiling, but then again, I often have a hard time understanding him. He keeps saying things that I think are supposed to be jokes, but I don't get why they're funny. It's hard to believe that it's almost been a year since he started tailing me.

What were we talking about? Oh, yes, Christmas. Since it's our first Christmas together, I wanted to do something special with them. I was thinking of traveling, maybe to New York or Paris or the moon. But, Nate wants to be home for Santa, Joey wants to go sledding, and Mary wants a big party with the whole extended family. And, technically, I am still under house arrest after last year's party (as well as most of the extended family), so I guess we'll be home for Christmas this year. I mean, we could sneak out, but then Mark would have to follow us and I don't want to make extra work for him over the holidays.

Mark thanked me for that when I told him. He also vetoed sledding, muttering something about 1/2 ton boys and collateral damage as he walked away. But, the next day he did bring a Christmas tree. It wasn't an old-fashioned aluminum one like Nate was hoping for, but a wooden one that looked like it might have grown that way. It's not what I would have chosen, but it's growing on me. I'm even starting to like the smell.

We've got a tree but what are we going to do? I've never had a Christmas without (most of) the whole family there, opening presents and out-doing each other with desserts. I want to make it special for the rob- - I mean, the kids - but I am at a total loss.

Mark hasn't been much help either. (I mean, other than the tree, of course. That was so thoughtful!) He's been rather mysterious lately. There have been a couple of time that I left the house, just to get his attention, and he wasn't even there. I asked him later where he had been, and he just grinned that grin of his. He does have really nice teeth. He told me that his parents are dentists, which makes sense to me. What was I saying? Yes - he just grinned and said "Christmas is coming, you know." Yes, Mark, I *do* know and that is why I am freaking out and no, Mark you didn't answer my question.

I had my suspicions, and flat out asked if he was following someone else on the side. Do you know what he said to that? "You're the only one for me, sweetheart." I'm getting better with his jokes and sarcasm, but that "sweetheart" thing really threw me off. I don't know what I was thinking - I replied "And don't you forget it, muffin!" *Muffin*? Really? Ugh - I'm so embarrassed.

Even though I don't know exactly what we're doing, I have been working on some gifts.

I've had to be pretty sneaky. Joey is such a snooper! I had 8 layers of encryption around the software patches, and he had broken through 7 when I caught him. I really don't want the surprise ruined for everyone. All of them have been bugging me for some new emotions. It's going to be a big responsibility, but I think they can handle it. Nate wants Joy, Joey wants Thrill, and Mary wants Romantic Love. They're almost done, but I've been having some trouble with Mary's. It's a little tricky programming feelings you don't have much experience in. We may need to debug later.

I'm a little stuck on Mark's present. It's not like me to wait until the last minute like this.

I just can't think of anything good enough for him.

Uh oh. I just got a text from Mark that he wants to talk to me about something important. I hope it's not that uranium I ordered - I really need that if I'm going to finish my other gifts on time.

OH. MY.

Pardon my poor punctuation. Grammar? I don't know. I'm flustered and flabbergasted and - wow. Let me catch my breath for a second.

So, Mark did start off with the uranium, but mid-scolding he smiled and did the strangest thing.

"Magdalena Alexandria Gretchen Svenson, I have never met another woman like you," he said. Of course, that's true. I do have pretty unique DNA. "You bring excitement to my life beyond what I ever could have imagined." Also true - he's a great guy, but not a "creative person."

"Mags, will you marry me?"

Then there was more jibber-jabber about me being smart and beautiful and whatnot - I think it's required to say those things when you're proposing, but I didn't fault him for it and decided to marry him anyway. The kids will be so excited!

It was Mark's idea to get married on Christmas, so we could have our first Christmas as a whole family. The extended family all participated by video call (except for my brother, whose reception has been spotty ever since he passed Mars' orbit.) Mark even surprised us with presents he made himself. There were the cookies, made from a mix and baked in a regular oven that tasted surprisingly similar to my "secret recipe." Then there were the scarves, knitted out of wool that were cozy, warm, and entirely legal. He also had a little bit of uranium for me, which was neither handmade nor entirely legal, but absolutely perfect.

Even with the impromptu wedding planning, I was still able to finish Mary's present, which turned out to be perfect timing. You see, since Mark felt that marrying the person he was supposed to be watching might be frowned upon by the FBI, he quit, and they sent a replacement. The replacement is a nice young man, new to the Bureau and quite attractive. We invited him to the wedding, and I'm afraid that Mary is quite smitten with young Anthony. We've forbidden any dating until she's at least a year, though, so we can work out any software bugs before things get serious. Mary is quite moody about it. She wants to get married at Christmas, just like Mom and Dad.

Andrew gets a little pale when she says that. Mark laughs, the boys tease, and I - well, I hope she gets her special Christmas, too, but I'm ok with waiting a year or two. They grow up so fast, you know? (But, I do know that sometimes a girl needs a little . . . help . . . and am working on a formula for pheromones for when she's ready.)

And, I finally figured out a gift for Mark! After he proposed, I asked what he wanted for Christmas and he said, "just your heart, sweetheart." So, I gave it to him.

I whipped up a quick artificial heart, based on the specifications on my own heart. He looked a little confused when he opened it, but after I explained, he kissed me and said he couldn't imagine a better gift.

If he thinks that's good, he needs to wait until next year. I've already planned what we're doing next Christmas, and he's going to love it! Well, as long as we survive the trip, but we maybe we just need a little Christmas magic to make it work.

About the Author

Loretta Jahncke lives in Wyoming, MI with her family. While she enjoys writing quirky stories, Loretta thinks her greatest talent is the ability to knit and read at the same time. Loretta spends her time driving teenagers around, hanging out with small children, grocery shopping, and telling people how to spell her name.

Adult Readers' Choice Winner
The Crossing
Will Miedema

"Could you tell us the story of your voyage, please?" Dr. Schulz asked from behind his desk. Thomas sat still for a few moments, listening to the hum of the fluorescent bulbs. "Again?" he asked.

"Again," said Schulz. "Our guest here is the esteemed Dr. Jacobsen, a pioneer in treating cases like yours. He's taken an interest in you, particularly. We're very honored to have him with us.

Thomas glanced at the visitor through thick horn-rimmed glasses. "All right," he sighed, "but I'm telling you right now, I don't need any bloody treatment. All I need is to get out of here. I never did what they said." "Just tell us what happened, please." said Schulz in his best I'm-the-expert-here voice. "Dr. Jacobsen truly believes we can be of help."

Thomas grunted, took a deep breath, and began to speak.

I left Liverpool in early November of 1946, with New York as my destination. I was told a November voyage was risky, though the ticketing agent assured me that the trip should take no more than 10 days in fair conditions.

My quarters were poor, though this didn't bother me much, as I didn't anticipate spending much time confined there anyway. The ship itself was dismal, each subsequent deck growing danker and darker as I descended. By the time I reached the lowest deck, the stench was near unbearable. No doubt a reflection of the scant fare I'd paid for the voyage.

The wind picked up slightly over the course of the first two days. No reason for concern, I was told by several seasoned sailors, though one of the younger men seemed worried. I wrote this off as youthful nerves—most of the veteran crew members seemed well at ease.

"Ain't nuffink to worry about," said the grizzliest sea dog of the group. "You'll learn to love a good sea breeze afore long."

A few days into the journey, I made an unlikely ally in the ship's cook. Our conversation flowed naturally, and though he was a bit rough around the edges (he had the telltale red nose of a man all too familiar with spirits), the unfortunately nicknamed Lumpy was easy to like.

As passengers and crew poured in for dinner, I offered to help serve the meal. He accepted, and we had a raucous time joking with passengers and cursing with the sailors. After the last remaining diners took their leave, we began cleaning up. Lumpy opened a bottle of rum to ease the passage of time and handed me a small glass.

"Thankee for the help. You'll be a full-timer in the galley 'afore long," He said, raising his glass.

I stayed for a while after the work was finished, content to listen to his stories. He frequently stopped to refill our glasses. Hours passed, and Lumpy's cheeks took on the same ruddy hue as his nose. I was feeling the effects of the rum myself, and knowing so, stood up to head back to my cabin.

"Jus' a min," said Lumpy, before I could leave. "Got sumptin' special for us to try. Won this one off'n some exotic stranger in a game o' dice. Strange fellow—didn't say much an' when 'e did was nigh impossible to unnerstan,' but paid up in the end, so how bad could e' be?"

He pulled out an ornate glass bottle, amber in color, and filigreed with hundreds of crawling salamanders, each one devouring the tail of the one in front of it.

"What is it?" I asked.

"Don't rightly know," said Lumpy, "but judgin' by the bottle, it weren't cheap." He uncorked it and poured two fingers of the liquid into each glass. We clinked them together and gulped the contents.

"Criminy," I said, coughing. "That pig piss is terrible."

"Bloody awful," he agreed, "reckon that sod cheated me after all." He nestled his large frame into a mound of russet potatoes and closed his eyes.

I chuckled and stumbled my way back to my cabin.

My headache upon waking was something to behold.

My pocketwatch indicated that the day was well into the afternoon, making me painfully aware of how hungry I was. A late lunch would also give me the opportunity to give Lumpy an earful about the swill he'd been tricked into.

I felt queasy, likely from the incessant rolling of the vessel. Despite the sailors' assurances, the wind hadn't died down in the slightest. Indeed, the weather had grown worse. The sky turned steel gray yesterday, and was even darker today, though no rain had yet begun to fall.

I threw off the bedsheets, noticing how damp they were. I had no memory of sweating so profusely in my sleep, but there was no mistaking the salty, tangy smell—strangely similar to that of the ocean. With how poor I was feeling at the moment, I wasn't particularly surprised.

I rose, only to be assaulted by a wave of nausea so powerful I immediately sank to the floor. I sat with my eyes closed for several minutes, breathing heavily, starting to sweat again. The queasiness in my stomach began to rise, creeping to the back of my throat. For an instant, I thought it would settle, and then I lost the ability to breathe. With a savage jerk, I wretched so violently I strained my neck.

A flood of what seemed like stagnant seawater erupted from my mouth, soaking the floorboards. I could breathe again, but I was in a state of pure panic. In the middle of a spreading puddle of slimy water wriggled a small purple salamander.

Not daring to stop and examine the wriggling creature I had coughed up, I sprinted to the galley.

I had to talk with Lumpy.

I didn't see Lumpy through the galley window, and I could tell that the sailors had to fend for themselves in his absence. Most of the sailors were unfazed—it was hardly the first time a cook with a liking for the bottle had slept through a meal. He'd turn up for dinner with a headache and an apologetic grin, just like before.

I nibbled some hardtack while I waited for the lingering crew members to leave. When they finally got up, I rifled through the galley, looking for the foul liquid from the night before. I thought of the purple amphibian lurking in my room and shuddered. What if something similar had happened to Lumpy?

My search was fruitless. No sign of Lumpy or the mysterious bottle. I turned to leave, scanning the room a final time with a sigh.

There!

One knife was missing from the block on the counter—the largest of the chef's knives, judging by the empty slot. Now I'm no cook, but in my youth, my mother reminded me constantly that a good chef always puts the knives away. Whether Lumpy was a good chef or not was certainly up for debate, but I knew he'd put the knives away once we finished our work.

So why was one missing? And where had Lumpy gone?

I grabbed the largest knife remaining in the block and left to find Lumpy's quarters.

Finding Lumpy's cabin was a struggle. There was no one below deck to point me in the right direction, and I wasn't used to the heightened rolling of the waves. Once, the heaving ship slammed me into a wall, causing me to cut my leg on the knife shoved in my pants. A dull drumming announced the arrival of the rain.

My nausea had settled, but had been replaced with a growing pain in my chest. I thought I could see a slight protuberance just below my sternum, but I shook this off as mad. I didn't trust my own mind after what had happened when I woke up.

At long last, I found the cabin reserved for the cook. I pressed my ear against the door, hoping to hear something through the gale battering the ship. Nothing.

I pried it open just enough to peek inside, but the black sky prevented any light from penetrating the gloom.

The hinges groaned in protest as I pushed the door open further. The room smelled of decay—dank and fetid, as if it had been overtaken by things that crawled and thrived in darkness. I pushed aside thoughts of the purple salamander. My chest quivered and ached. In a moment of brave stupidity, I beat my fist against my sternum, thinking I'd subject my body to my will. My vision exploded in a flash of lavender light, bringing me to my knees.

Crouched on all fours, partially out of blinding pain, partially due to the heaving ship, I explored Lumpy's cabin, groping in the darkness.

There was nothing there. No Lumpy, no bottle.

I slammed my fist on the floor in anger, then cursed as something bit deeply into my hand. Warmth ran down my fingers as blood poured from the wound. What had I struck? I rose to my feet, swaying with the motion of the boat as I scuffled my feet on the floor, seeking out what had cut me.

I kicked something—a metallic clang rose above the roar of the storm. Crouching again, more carefully this time, I felt along the rough floorboards until my good hand closed around a cold steel handle.

Lumpy's kitchen knife.

The first flash of lightning that pierced the goom threatened to overload my senses, but in the instant that it came and went, the cabin was illuminated. At least five salamanders slithered to find the safety of darkness.

The flashing increased in frequency, each time offering a moment's vision. The brightest flash yet revealed Lumpy's knife was covered in black sludge, crusted and dried, corroding the tempered steel edge.

I clenched Lumpy's large blade in my good hand, and ignoring the raging fire in the other, drew the smaller knife I had taken. I bolted from the room, not daring to look behind me as I slammed the door.

I couldn't go back to my cabin—not without telling someone else what was going on—and I wasn't ready to face any more salamanders just yet—not after seeing more of them in Lumpy's quarters. I had to go to the Captain.

The wind and waves had become so fierce that I practically crawled to the bridge, leaving bloody scrapes in my wake. I met no one, but assumed all hands were on deck battling the storm.

The bridge was sparse, populated only by the Captain and the navigator, who both looked up sharply upon my entrance. My grisly appearance did nothing to set them at ease.

"What are you doing here?" asked the Captain, clearly exhausted.

As I opened my mouth to speak, I retched again, heaving at the captain's feet. No seawater or creatures this time, just my hardtack.

"Bollocks, boy!" he cried, "pull it together and tell me why you're yawning in technicolor on my bridge!"

Before I could talk, the door burst open and the first mate, a man named Johnson, entered, chest heaving.

"We found Lumpy, Cap'n. He's...er....dead, sir. Murdered by the look of it. Thomas found him stowed in the galley pantry. Had a hole in his chest, and was near unrecognizable from all manner of gashes and slashes."

I groaned. How could I forget to check the pantry?

The Captain looked at me with raised eyebrows. Johnson followed his gaze, now noticing my presence.

"Who's this? What's he doing..." He noticed my blood-stained clothes and the knives still in my, dry with gore.

"YOU!" he snarled.

I dropped the knives and held up my hands in what I hoped was a gesture of innocence. "You don't understand," I said, "that's why I came to the Captain. There's something happening on the ship."

"Came to kill the Cap'n too, more like." He turned to the Captain, "We can't have this nutter on our ship anymore, he's a threat to the entire crew. Lost his mind, he has."

The Captain grunted, turning to me. "You won't be any more trouble." It wasn't a question. "Lock him in his cabin. We'll deliver him to the authorities when we arrive in New York."

My cabin reeked, but apart from the wet floor, there was no indication of unwelcome company. My salamander friend had either escaped or was hiding. I tried the lock, but they had found a way to lock it from the outside.

The lump in my chest had grown, without question. I recalled what Johnson said about Lumpy and the hole in his chest. I had a sickening suspicion about what was happening, leaving me only one course of action.

I rifled through my belongings, seeking anything that could work. Despair settled in as my search revealed nothing. If only I hadn't left Lumpy's knives back at the bridge!

I kicked the leg of the tiny writing desk in rage, splintering it off in a jagged end. Picking up the sharpened stake, I scanned the cabin for the other missing piece. Ultimately, I decided my best bet was the blunt end of another desk leg.

Turning the two wooden limbs over in my hands, I couldn't help but grimace. A crude hammer and chisel. This was going to be agony.

I opened the door to the water closet and peeled off my crusted shirt, cringing at the sight of the angry red bulge. Whatever it was, it had to come out, and I wasn't about to let it stay in my room.

Hunching over the toilet, I pressed the sharpened table leg against the mass. The cramped stall left me little room for precision. I braced myself, held my breath, and pounded the stake into the wound.

I couldn't breathe through the blinding misery, but I could see, and what I saw I will remember in my nightmares forever.

Black sludge poured from the gash, rancid beyond belief, but nothing was fouler than the squirming mass that wriggled around the bowl of the toilet, scrambling for purchase, looking for the safety of darkness. I jabbed it in horror, forcing it deeper into the plumbing with the desk leg that had just been used to set it free.

I clambered out of the tiny bathroom to grab anything I might use to stop up the opening in the toilet. Grabbing my packed clothes and towels, I jammed them firmly into place with what fading strength I had left. Not content, I stacked everything I could on top of the toilet lid, then blocked the bathroom door with the dresser.

Panting heavily, I flopped onto the bed. I was still in immense pain, but it was pain I was sure I could survive. I fell asleep thinking my situation had improved.

It had not.

A slap to the face brought me rudely awake. My mouth was gagged, my hands and feet tied. First mate Johnson sneered at me cruelly, surrounded by four other sailors I'd seen, but whose names I didn't know.

"He's awake, boys," he laughed. He made no attempt at silence, nor did he need to. The storm still raged outside, loud enough to mask all but the loudest of noises. What little sound I could produce had no chance of being heard, and I doubted there were any who would care, anyway.

"Smells like a sty in here, lad. Wot you been up to?"

I tried to answer, and the men laughed at my muffled attempt to speak.

"Cap'n says you're making it to shore, but I says you ain't. As I sees it, you're the source o' all our troubles. Bad luck to keep a dead man on board. Worse yet to keep his killer." he licked his lips and flashed a feral smile. "Grab him, lads. We'll see how strong 'a swimmer he is."

None of the men protested. I flailed, trying to get loose, but I was no match for the hardened sailors and their years of physical toil.

The clamor of the wind and rain was deafening—that the men kept their feet while carrying me across the deck spoke to their experience at sea.

"Over the side and let's be done with it!" Johnson roared to be heard over the sound of the squall. They staggered toward the railing, leaning into the wind, maintaining their vice-like grip.

I fell as if in slow motion. Lightning flashed, and in an eerie moment, I saw my own reflection hurtling toward the water.

My last memory was of hitting the water and thinking, "I'm free."

"What do you make of it?" asked Schulz, after Thomas had been dismissed. "His story? Complete nonsense," said Jacobsen.

"Parts of it make sense, do they not? What of the scars on his hand and chest?"

"Self-mutilation, most likely. A perfect example of psychosis. The mind invents an escape to avoid dealing with reality. Hallucinations, delusions, self-harm; it's textbook. How did he get here?"

"Someone found him on the beach. He was initially taken for dead, but the police were contacted once it was discovered he was still alive." Schulz scratched his two-day stubble absently. "What do you think about treatment?"

"Normally I'd recommend insulin therapy, but that's fallen out of favor ever since a new procedure has made its way from Europe. An operation that transforms the unstable into docile, functional members of society again. Have you heard of this?"

"I haven't. You've performed such an operation?"

"I have, to marvelous effect. If you agree, I can perform it on Thomas."

Schulz thought for a moment. "I'll check the schedule with Eunice so we can clear a morning for while you're still in town."

"Excellent." Jacobsen smiled a rather wolfish smile. "Congratulations, Dr. Schulz. Your facility is about to have its first lobotomy patient."

About the Author

Will Miedema was born and raised in West Michigan, but he's definitely going to die in Florida. After getting his B.A. in History from Michigan State University, he took brief stints in construction, customer service, and tech support before landing in marketing, where he's been ever since. He's currently a copywriter and content manager in the software industry, and picks up the occasional freelance gig when time allows. He's also working on his first novel, but don't ask him how it's going. In his free time, he enjoys electric guitars, mountain biking, and making pizza. Will lives in Rockford, MI, with his wife and two children.

Adult Published Finalist

Prismatic Sun
Julie Foust

We sped out into the desert. No road ahead of us. The driver dodged the larger rocks and debris that were scattered across the landscape. There was a deeply melancholy feeling in my chest as I looked out over what used to be home. The buildings are gone. So are the trees, and anything green. Everything is slowly turning to dust. And soon, so shall I.

I know we are getting close. I don't have much time left. The dawn is rising and chasing the shadows away and we head straight toward it. I suspect They haven't yet moved into place. I was told I wouldn't see sunlight again, but here are the faintest traces of it brightening the sky before me. The stars are beginning to disappear on the horizon. That is more than I could have hoped for.

"Dammit, wer late! Wer 'unna haff to do this fast now, Loverboy!" The driver said.

Warren didn't move. His eyes were glued straight ahead. He hadn't said a word to me since the ceremony the night before. I didn't know what he was thinking. He didn't speak. He didn't move. It was as if I was travelling to my death with a statue as a companion. But of course, I didn't know what to say. I couldn't speak to him either. I knew what he had to do and I could see the terror behind his blank stare. I wondered if he was angry at me for all of this? It wasn't my fault. They chose him! I didn't pick him. I don't *think* I picked him. But if I had to choose one person to spend my last moments with, it would be him.

But he hasn't looked me in the eyes. Not that he ever really did before.

The driver bangs his fist on the dashboard, impatient at ninety miles per hour.

I gaze out the window at the last few sturdy walls of a collapsed motel that I used to pass every day on my way to school. And the ruins of the grocery store where Mom bought food on her way home. And the ashy husk of city hall. It was over. They came and They drove us underground. We didn't have a chance, but maybe we do now.

Suddenly the light that I had noticed creeping over the horizon disappeared. The whole sky turned a menacing pitch black. All of the stars were gone and the horizon was no longer visible at all. The driver now had to rely entirely on the van's headlights to guide us.

"Start op'ning the boxes!" The driver shouted. Neither of us moved.

"Didja fuckin' hear me? Start op'ning the boxes! We're late!"

I looked over at Warren. He did not move. I leaned down to the container between us and opened it to reveal five plain white gift boxes with each of our initials stamped on them. Three of them are smaller than the other two. They are all separated and secured with duct tape to the edge of the container.

Traditionally, there is a driver, there is a man, there is a woman. Traditionally, the driver comes back. This time, he won't. But we have to keep up the façade. They could be watching from anywhere on the surface.

Two packages are customary. The extra three are our own special plan. Our people's plan. We don't know if it will work. But we have no other choice. We are going to die anyway, so why not try to make it count? And if we succeed? They die or They decide to leave our people alone. If we fail? Maybe nothing will happen. Or maybe They will catch on to our plan and kill everyone on the planet. They could. All this sacrifice shit is just Them toying with us. They could destroy our whole solar system if They wanted to.

But instead, twice a year They assign a driver, a man, and a woman to go to the surface. The man and the woman never come back. And the drivers never last too long. Driving people to their death takes its toll. They last three years at most. This is our driver's fourth year. He won't be coming back. He will get scooped up like the rest of us.

He is ready for it. You can just feel it. The way he acts is like an outlaw on death row. Reckless and dangerous. But still, in a way, determined. There is a fire in this driver. I wouldn't be surprised if his last words are "I'm unna get you suns-a-bitches!" But that is something only he will ever know.

"I see it!" He yells. "Them boxes open? Hand me my gun!" The driver always gets a gun.

So does the man.

The woman gets shot in the head. In the right place, if she is lucky.

Then the driver kills the man, positions the bodies, and then drives away.

This time, he wont drive away. This time, the driver will, hopefully, be hitching a ride with the dead bodies of the man and the woman, Warren and me. We will be dead. No way to get around that. Our people had already tried that the first year. They have to be dead, or we get punished. The great cosmic mystery of death forced upon us for the good of our people. In a few minutes Warren and I would know the answer to that mystery. Heaven or nothingness? Pain or numbness? What does it feel like to die?

The driver will be the one to detonate the explosives in the three white boxes. Those were the boxes I had started opening first. When the driver started to yell for his gun, I fumbled with the larger package stamped with H.C. My hands were shaking, and my mouth was dry and I couldn't find the words to answer the driver as he continued to yell for his gun.

Suddenly, Warren's hands were on mine. He steadied my shaking and helped pull the gun out of the box once I had it open. He handed it forward to the driver. He turned back to the container and took the box I was still clinging to out of my hands and dropped it back inside. He picked up the one explosive watch I had managed to free from its gift box before the driver had yelled to me. Warren strapped the watch to his arm. He opened another of the small boxes and strapped that watch to my wrist. He got the last one ready for the driver, but did not put it on him yet. I could tell he was waiting until the driver stopped banging his fists on the dashboard.

Warren didn't touch the last box. His gun. He just held on to the last watch and stared forward again.

The driver slowed as we approached the alter. The "alter."

It was a stone pit filled with sand. There were four pillars surrounding it that served as markers so we could distinguish it from the rest of the desolate, sandy landscape. The driver drove slightly past it and then backed up through the pillars to the pit itself. When he stopped the car, Warren handed him his watch.

"Hey, thanks man." The driver glanced at me and shook his head. "Every time. The women are always the ones that lose it."

I was still shaking, but his comment made me straighten up. I was frightened, but I didn't want to be. I didn't want to "lose it". I'm the calm one. I never lose it. Especially not around Warren.

I wish he would look at me. I just want to look into his eyes. Tell him I'm sorry even though I haven't done anything wrong. Kiss him and tell him it will be okay. But he rarely looked me in the eyes before. And I've never kissed him. Only wanted to. And he knows it. He's known about my feelings for him for years. Maybe that is why I am sure he blames me. But I was devastated when They called his name at the ceremony. I don't want him to die. He is a ray of sunshine in our underground world and now that light will be gone. Even if our plan works and They leave, I feel sorry for everyone who will never hear his laugh again. Selfishly, though, I am the slightest bit grateful that he will be the last person I see, but I would have never chosen him, if I had been given a choice.

He never liked me, though. Or maybe he did. He never told me. He never made a move, but he never turned me down, either. Nothing ever happened. And now we are going to die together and he still hasn't said a word about any of it. We only have minutes left to live and I am more afraid that I will never know how he feels about me. How stupid is that? I'm better than that, aren't I?

But still, regret fills me. Would there have been sparks, like I always imagined there would be? Or absolutely nothing, validating my worry that I had wasted so many years pining after the wrong man? I just wish I knew. What would it feel like to kiss him?

I took a few deep breaths and reached for the door handle. It took me a few seconds, but I finally convinced myself to get out of the van. I looked up to where the stars should be and saw only black. I took a few more deep breaths, but then I caught a whiff of cigarette smoke from the driver, who was just staring off in the direction of the horizon. Avoiding the smoke, I moved around the back of the van and to the other side where Warren was. He was fiddling with the watch on his wrist, and staring at the box that contained his gun.

He still hadn't opened it. I moved a little closer.

Didn't he see me?

His gaze doesn't waiver. He stares at the box. The van's dome light illuminates just enough of his features for me to tell he is angry. More angry than I have ever seen him.

I take another step toward him. And another. And I place my hand on his arm and he still doesn't move.

"Hey! You two! It's startin'! Get goin'! And couldja do it in the pit? I don't have time to be doin' any draggin'!

I bent down to look through the windshield of the van. I could see the horizon line again.

It was still the deepest black, but now what we called the Prismatic Sun rose. Squares of light and color flashed, both blinding and mesmerizing. They spun around, creating the illusion of a sun-like sphere rising in the distance. I could not see beyond the colors, though I knew there must be some sort of ship behind them. It rose much more quickly than the sun.

"Didja fuckin hear me? This ain't a peepshow! We got a job to do."

I turned to look at Warren. He had bent to look though the windshield like I had, but he stayed bent and stared at the gun box again. He slowly picked it up and opened it.

I felt sick. I walked away toward the pit, stopped at the trunk and looked back. Warren was holding the gun.

"Time to go, bud. We're 'unna fuck Their shit up!"

Warren leaned into the van, and said something to the driver that I couldn't quite hear. "We don't have a fuckin' minute!" the driver exclaimed. His tone softened for what he said next. "But I'll give you a few seconds to say goodbye in private," the driver took Warren's free hand and shook it, and then continued sternly, "so's long as you do it in the fuckin' pit!"

Warren broke the handshake and turned quickly to me. When he got close to me, he looked toward me, but not at me. He gave me a regretful smirk as his gun twitched in his hand. I turned and walked into the pit. I knew as soon as I stepped in that he could do it any second.

Every step I took, I flinched thinking it would be my last. But I reached the middle of the pit and turned around to see Warren standing just a foot away. I could see his face clearly in the bright, colorful, flashing light of the Prismatic Sun.

There was anger and sadness and regret and pity and defeat all reflected in his eyes. I took his hand in mine before I had even realized my own hand was moving. Tears formed in both of our eyes. He tore his hand free.

His eyes met mine. He said, "I'm sorry."

I saw the driver appear from the other side of the van, just as Warren leaned in and kissed me, softly, on the lips.

My eyes closed.

I didn't feel a thing.

About the Author

Julie Anna Foust is a 28-year-old Earth female who recently graduated from Ferris State University with a Bachelor's degree in History. She is a film buff, amateur photographer, and a collector of many things including novelty drinking glasses and vinyl records. She has always enjoyed writing in many different forms, but only recently began to consider it as a serious hobby. This is the first of her works that has been read by the public.

Adult Published Finalist

Show Me How to Feel the Stars
Chris Sorenson

Playful giggles and screams filled the early evening air. Pop-tops cracked open with metallic clacking, while hamburgers and hotdogs sizzled, noisily and deliciously fragrant on the grill. Children and adults of all ages and relation played and bantered on the back deck, overlooking neatly kept gardens and the churning waters of the in-ground pool.

The girl sat at one shaded corner of the deck sipping warm Kool-Aid and trying to wash away the taste of chlorinated pool water from her mouth. She was not having fun. Her body quivered as drops of water fell from her bare arms and hair, soaking the large towel that engulfed her body. She listened dejectedly as a few children still sniggered cautiously from the pool.

"She makes a really good Marco." she heard one girl bray. "Marco-Polo!" a boy whispered.

"Why don't you shut up? That was really mean what you did, you know. She swallowed a lot of water!" another young voice hissed.

"Pffffttt, she shouldn't be in the pool anyway, she just gets in our way." the first girl retorted.

Turning away from the voices and frowning, the girl swallowed another sip through a thick throat and stood. Feeling her way methodically along familiar wood and furniture, she made it to a sliding glass door. She stepped inside and slammed the door loudly behind her. Other jovial voices inside stopped their chatter abruptly at the racket. Her wet feet slapped the vinyl floor as the girl hurried to her room, face wet again, but not from dripping hair. A woman's voice trailed behind her "Honey? Everything alright?" The girl did not answer and the woman's voice was cut short by the slamming of the bedroom door.

She could still hear giggles and screams outside her window. Her face buried deeply in her wet pillow she tried fruitlessly to muffle the sounds of fun. Then, from the hallway she heard the shuffling of familiar footsteps, followed by a soft knock.

"Not right now!" The girl shouted toward the door.

Despite her tearful appeal the door opened anyway. Shuffling steps approached her bed and she felt the person sit down. Lifting her head, she knew right away who it was. She could smell the scent of lingering pipe smoke and the faint but familiar aroma of shaving lotion. Her chest hitched slightly, but she managed. "Hi, Grampa. I didn't think you were coming today."

"I didn't either, but I got feeling better as the day went on and decided I could make it. I wanted to visit you today and I never want to miss a chance for fireworks."

"Thanks, I'm glad you're here." the girl said sitting up in her bed. "I heard you were having a bit of a rough afternoon?" he inquired.

"I don't really want to talk about it, just some stupid kids. I don't even know why they got invited."

Her grandfather shifted his weight to the edge of the bed, leaning forward to retrieve something from the floor. There was the rustle of nylon and the sound of what seemed like a mile-long zipper being undone. A brief rustle again and then he spoke.

"Scoot over here. Hold out your hands. I brought something for you to have. It always cheers me up."

The girl did as she was asked, holding out her hands eagerly as she had many times before. His gifts rarely, if ever, disappointed. He laid it carefully in her arms, taking time to be sure she had a firm grip before letting it go. Cradling the gift for a moment, the girl was unsure about how to proceed with such a foreign object.

"What is it, Grampa?

"Tell me what you feel."

Running her hand over the object, she carefully inspected it. She felt both its distinct smooth curves and sharply bent lines. It was not heavy and felt well balanced in her arms. She tapped with her fingernail on what she perceived to be the objects top. The soft resonance of thinly shaved yet rigid wood rang pleasantly beneath. Allowing her left hand to travel up and over the rest of the object she felt it smooth and rounded until her hand traced over four cool metal mechanisms vastly different from the rest of the object.

"I know what it is!" she said smiling. "Thank you so much."

"Well, tell me what you think it is then!" he responded a chuckle in his voice.

Instead of answering, she let her fingers move along the object for a moment more until she found what she was searching for. Once she did, she stuck out her thumb and let it rake across four tightly stretched strings allowing them to ring forth in a twangy-bright harmony.

"Where did you get it, Grampa? I love it!"

"I brought it back from Hawaii many years ago when I was in the service.

It's been in one closet or another for the past sixty years, but it's still in great shape. I put new strings on it for you and tuned it up."

"It has a beautiful sound. Can you play it?"

"Sure, hand it over."

He gently lifted it from her arms, grasping the tiny neck with his large, aging hand while his fingers landed naturally along the frets. He immediately began to strum. A brilliant ringing of bright chords filled her bedroom. It sent a wave of tingles up the girls back that traveled directly to her lips bending them up in a grin. Then to her great surprise he began to sing over his strumming in a foreign language. He repeated a few lines, his voice undulating from high to low in smooth tones then ending in a jovial vibrato.

"That's all I know!" He laughed. "I picked that one up from the base!"

"It sounded happy!"

"I don't even remember what the words mean now, but I always loved that little Hawaiian melody. It never fails to make me feel good."

"Me too."

"If you put the time into practicing, you'll be good on it in no time, you already have a great ear for music, and you have a wonderful voice."

"Thanks, and I will, I love it."

"What do you say you help me up and we go eat now? I want to get filled up before they start the fireworks."

"Ok" she said, standing up to help.

Young and old alike ooohed and ahhhhed as the sky erupted with thousands of bright sparks and colorful trails of fire. Children gasped and threw their hands over their ears as whistles, crackles and booms rang through the air. Smoke crept over dew covered lawns and lingered in the air like a low fog. A few mosquitos buzzed lazily after the show. The girl sat on her bench with her eyes closed, quietly listening to the display and the screams of others around her. She clapped with everyone at the finale but remained on her bench as the crowd began to depart. Still later, she sat as her grandfather joined her.

"Can I sit with you a while by the fire?"

"Sure."

"The fireworks were fun tonight. Did you enjoy them?" he said sitting down.

"Ya, I guess. They were really loud and smokey."

"It's going to be a beautiful night. I bet there will be a million stars over our heads tonight when we go to bed."

"Grampa, that makes me sad to think about."

"What makes you sad?"

"Thinking about seeing the stars."

"Why child? It shouldn't."

 She did not answer, and he did not press.

The dying fire rolled peacefully in its small backyard pit, casting a warm glow onto the faces of the girl and her grandfather. They sat quietly and alone for a while, listening to the crackle and occasional popping of pitch within the smoldering logs. Fragrant smoke intwined with the evening's gentle breeze and drifted silently past noses keen to the world around them. A few distant crickets chirped their nightly serenade. There was a faint hitching of her chest and a sniffle from the girl. The old man raised his head toward the endless night sky. Thousands of shimmering jewels, beyond anyone's reach but free to all below, shone across the sky as he spoke softly.

"You do not need your sight to experience the world around you, especially the stars. They are there for everyone."

Feeling the warmth of flannel and weathered hands wrap lovingly around her shoulder, she lifted her downturned head. For an instant, fire light flickered on the tiny diamond droplets in her unseeing eyes before being blinked away. In nearly a whisper, her small voice, still thick from ebbing tears, asked, "How can I ever *experience* something I can't feel with my other senses? I can never feel the stars"

"I'll show you how, give me your hand," the old man said.

He took her hand gently in his, opening her palm toward the heavens. "I'll show you how to feel the stars."

In the girl's up-turned palm he touched three times and then connected the dots with the swipe of his finger.

"Do you know what that is?" he asked.

"No."

"That Orion's belt. Orion is a hunter that watches over us in the night sky. You'll know he's above when the weather starts to get cold. When you feel the cool nip and the snow on your nose at night he's there.

"Where is he now?" the girl asked.

"In the summer, he rises just before dawn to check on all the sleeping people in their beds, even us."

The girl raised her head toward the sky opening her eyes wide. "Show me another?"

He took her hand again and gently traced a square with four dots. Stemming from each corner, he drew four jutting and bent lines.

"What's that one?" she asked.

"That's the keystone of Hercules. He favors the night sky when the weather is warm like tonight. When you hear the crickets and peepers and the mosquitos buzz around your ears, you'll know he's looking down."

The man pursed his lips and made a whooshing sound brushing the girl's hair back as he did.

"That was a burning meteorite falling to the earth. A shooting star!"

The girl giggled, squirming away then back into a warm embrace. She felt the familiar warmth of his body and his scent as he hugged her. Resting her head for a while, she listened through his flannel shirt to the faint slow thumping of his old heart. Nestling her ear deeper into his chest, she wondered for the first time just how many times his old heart had beat. A million? A billion? As many as the stars?

"I've got another one for you, hold out your hand again," he said.

She held out her palm again and he took her hand. With a finger he traced a long zigzagging line in her soft flesh from her wrist to the tip of her longest finger. Within the line he made many dots. "This is Hydra hssssss" he said with a playful little hiss. The girl drew her hand back a bit but he held it firmly.

"Don't be afraid, I won't bite," he chuckled. "But I'll save that story for another fire some night. Hydra is the largest constellation in the entire sky. It comes out when you can start to smell the first hints of spring in the air."

"Do you mean like the smell of the snow melting or the flowers starting to come out?"

"That's exactly right, don't you just love that time of year!"

"Yes, but how did you learn about all of this, there are so many."

"My father taught me many of them when I was young. He taught me so many things."

"Did you sit with your dad by campfires?"

"Oh yes, hundreds. We would talk for hours sometimes. He sure would have loved you and all the funny things you come up with."

Closing her eyes tightly she listened to the dying fire and remembered the lesson. She thought about what it would have been like to sit with her great-grandfather by a fire and her grandfather as just a boy her age. She smiled at the thought.

Holding out her palm, she drew Orion marking each star in the belt firmly then adding the line just as her grandfather had. She shivered a bit when she thought of the cold air that the fall and winter would bring when Orion would be in the night sky above. It seemed like ages away when she thought of all the warm summer nights still ahead, listening to her grandfather's lessons and stories. Some of his stories might be serious or even scary, but she never forgot them and she always felt better listening to him talk. Sometimes she would simply drift off at the fireside, or, in the winter, on the warmth of the couch, only to wake up in her bed in the morning with good fresh thoughts in her head. Tonight, she decided, however, that she could listen all night.

"I've got one more for you. Hold out your hand. Make it into a cup," he said holding back a grin.

She heard the slightest smile in his voice and the crackle of a plastic bottle as his hand found hers. Then before she knew it, her hand was filled with the ice-cold water from his bottle. It ran down between her fingers and onto her bare toes taking her breath away.

"That's the big dipper!" he said, roaring with laughter.

High giggles and hearty old laughter erupted into the still night. Even the peepers with their shrill, persistent call paused for the slightest moment, as if to let the two enjoy their laugh. Finally, when the last of the laughter and joking subsided, they sat again as they had before, two silent figures, feeling the fire and thinking good thoughts.

Later, with the remains of the fire dwindling to coals a woman's voice called from the house.

"Daaaaad? Your ride's here. Need some help coming in?"

"No thanks, I've got my navigator sitting right next to me!" the old man replied nudging the girl playfully with his elbow.

"Here, Grandpa. Let me help you up." the girl said, getting to her feet.

"Thank you honey." he said "You know your way better than anyone, you're the best guide I could ask for."

Together they walked to the house in the darkness of the night, one blind from birth, the other from old age. Yet, knowing every obstacle, the girl led her grandfather flawlessly as she held his hand. High above, the stars shone down upon them, twinkling like diamonds.

About the Author

Chris Sorenson is a lifelong resident of southeast Michigan where he lives with his wife and two young children. His children inspire him to tell and write fictional stories with strong young lead characters. Chris was involved in collegiate flight training for over fifteen years where he made contributions to flight training journals and various scholarly writing. He now lives in Ann Arbor where he owns and operates a banjo making business that supplies parts and banjos sold all over the world. In his spare time, he enjoys writing fiction for young readers and is nearly finished with his first novel.

Adult Published Finalist

Riparian Zones
K.S. Walker

SUNDAY

"You haven't forgiven me yet, have you?"

After all we've been through the past week, I can see how easily it would be to tell Donté yes. Because nothing he's done will change that I believe he will be a caring and attentive father to the child hiccupping in my belly. Because Donté has always believed me, believed in me, and that hasn't changed either. We fit together, Donté and I, like the canopy line of hardwood trees; we've always left space for the other to grow into. I can imagine the ease of settling into life together again. But it wouldn't be the same, would it? My wound might heal, but the glass shard would still be there, waiting to be bumped and rupture the newest scar tissue.

I shake my head no.

"Will you ever?"

Instead of answering I take his hand. We watch the ocean stretch out in front of us, vast and rippling in the moonlight. The only thing I can hear is the sound of waves breaking against the shore, none of the wailings of grief, ferocity or acceptance that I had grown used to. I wonder what kind of co-parents we'll be and if we can be friends again one day. But also, if this what it's supposed to feel like, letting go? Like warm licks of water against your toes? Like buoyant possibility?

SATURDAY

I know it's time. The merfolk is singing the same lonely song for the fourth time this morning. It's different from the first song I heard that drew me off trail, wading into the swampy floodplains in search of the creature that could sing so beautifully about surrender. This song carries an urgency to its rhythm, ushering me on to accept the inevitable.

I sit at the edge of the bathtub, trailing my hand through the warm water. The creature blinks at me, curiously, knowingly, before swimming to brush up against my palm. I can feel the smooth ridges where scales were missing from its flank. The injury itself, though, is healed. It strokes its four-clawed hands against my wrist gently. I'm more than three times the size of the merfolk, but I hold no pretenses. We're both aware of the amount of damage those talons could inflict. This, however, is not a warning but a gentle supplication: *Release. Release.*

Donté does not hesitate, when I ask him once more for help. It's nearing midnight when the car is loaded up. We drive eastward listening to podcasts about climate change and sustainability. About old-growth forests and riparian zones. About how wetlands both slow the velocity of floodwaters and the steady march of erosion. And can you imagine being so mighty? Several times he presses pause so we can talk about what we're hearing. The conversation flows so naturally between us it pierces the soft spots I've left exposed.

FRIDAY

I am back to avoiding phone calls.

I am also avoiding the upstairs bathroom.

Instead of returning home after a half-day setting up my classroom, I pick up a sandwich and drive out to the big lake.

After Mom left, my dad would take my sister and me to the lakeshore. Those days it was almost a three hour drive with all the bathroom stops. My sister, you couldn't keep out of the water. She'd swim for hours, begging Dad to pick her up and toss her in, only for her to emerge moments later and yell 'Again!' But I spent my time on the safety of the shore letting the shallow waves lap at my feet. I'd comb the pebbly beach for blue-green winks of beach glass edges rounded smooth.

I eat my sandwich on a drying piece of driftwood. Watching couples watch their dogs frolicking in the waves. Commotion at the shoreline catches my attention.

A group of children are squatting around something in the sand. Now two of them are arguing and a third is poking at something with a stick. My heart catches in the back of my throat, worried about what they might have found. I waddle over to them as quickly as I can given the sand, but also I don't want to alarm their parents--wherever they are.

"What'd you guys find there?" I ask as I approach. I am puffing as I reach them and I try to hide the panic in my voice.

The one with the stick stands, and the two that were bickering quiet. Caught in the shallow pool is a small walleye. No copper-wire patches of hair, no wide flat full-moon face. No pearlescent purple-grey body fused to shining blue-mist scales. The walleye is alive still but just barely.

"The right thing to do, would be to get it back in the water, yeah?" All three children nod. I smile uncertainly, and leave them.

THURSDAY

Steeled by my conversation with Corrinne, I pick up the phone to call my father back. It's the bravest thing I've done in so long and I'm exhausted before he even answers. But when he does I'm so relieved to hear his voice, and its familiar cadence that at first I don't quite realize what he's saying. I'm shocked into silence as he continues: He tells me that he still loves me, but he doesn't think it's right. That love is not selfish and real marriages take work. And it's not right to keep a man from his child. And I know he's not just talking to me when he says this.

I don't know how to tell him that this love he has to offer is dry rot eating at me from the inside out.

I don't know how to tell him that I am not my mother.

I don't know how to tell him that I've already lost Donté, I can't lose him too.

Before long my muffled sobs are lost in the crescendo of the song the merfolk is singing in the bathroom. It understands my grief in a way I have yet to, and it sings it back to me. I curl next to the bathtub and rock and wail to the melodies that carry me like foam on waves.

The song echoes through me long after it ends. The merfolk looks at me with large unblinking eyes, surprisingly bright. And then it does two flips and swims away. I've never seen anything more agile in my life. In its beach-glass eyes I read a question that I just cannot answer yet.

WEDNESDAY

The merfolk is moving better than it was yesterday. It stays very still, beneath the water, waiting, perhaps, for the minnows to forget there is a predator among them, and then it springs forward, wide jaws snapping. Sometimes it uses its claws to meticulously peel ribbons of flesh from its prey rather than eating it whole. There is a specific song it sings after a successful hunt. Three short trills followed by a long undulating note that is still raining down around me when Corinne calls.

She's been giving me space. I appreciate it, but I can't escape the twinge of guilt I feel at not having contacted her first.

"Why didn't you tell me you've seen Donté?" is the first thing she says.

"I don't want to talk about Donté," I say standing, and wiping my hands on my jeans. "Because he called me yesterday. He told me to tell you how sorry he was and he'd take it all back..." Corrinne stops. "Did he hit you, Lee?"

The concern in her voice wrings me dry. Is this what my sister has been thinking since I've left her in radio silence? "He didn't hit me."

Corinne's relief is palpable. "Did he cheat? Because if you need me to bust a broad's kneecaps I'll bust some kneecaps."

And like that Corinne has coaxed out my first laugh in days. The sound is foreign to me, ricocheting off the bathroom tiles. Corinne is a doctoral student in Feminist Studies and has never been in a physical altercation in her life--she'd never. Besides, all this would've been easier if he did cheat. Simpler at least.

"Everybody keeps their kneecaps," I pause, uncertain of how much to say. But this is Corinne I'm talking to. "He threw away the ultrasound pictures, Corinne. From before."

I brace for her to tell me I'm overreacting. That I had no business getting pregnant at nineteen and no business keeping those photos all this time.

She'd never, but I build the levees anyway. Just in case.

"Lee...I--I'm so, so sorry." Her sympathies fill me like a well. My eyes are brimming over.

"Don't tell Dad. I haven't told Dad yet."

"Lee, call him. Call Dad back, okay? Do you need me? I can come over right, now--"

What I want more than anything is to fold myself in my sister's arms and have her tell me everything will be okay. But I can't risk her being near the merfolk. There's a fine for harboring them now and a threat of jail time. Perhaps I am selfish, but not so selfish.

"No, no. I'll call you back later okay?"

"Okay," she says, "I love you." She pauses before she says, "You and your babies". And then she hangs up.

TUESDAY

The forums surprise me. I expected nothing more than thread after thread expressing shallow interest in exploitation of merfolk for celebrity and profit. Instead I find theories both scientific and spiritual. Some people are saying evolution made a leap while we weren't looking, perhaps somewhere dark and unknowable, away from meddling human eyes. I've heard others are calling them our ancestors, questioning the link between humans and primates.

I'm primed to believe I'm looking into our past as I'm feeling this child do swish-flips in my belly. After all, whales and hippos are close cousins. And that two-legged kick-push newborns do? Maybe it'd get them somewhere if it wasn't for all this gravity and dry land. But all I know for sure is that I'd get a $500 check for calling the DNR tip line.

I've also read that there are ghost restaurants with secret menus offering sirène au vin and ningyo tempura rolls--you just have to know who to ask. User @finsforfinley suggests that they've got to get their supply from somewhere.

Despite how our last conversation ended, Donté shows up before work, like he said he would, with containers full of minnows and crawfish. This creature in my bathroom is an intelligent predator, Donté tells me. It might not be any longer than my forearm, but a swarm of them could take down a great white shark to feed its family. Or so they say. It seems we've been reading the same forums. We can only begin to imagine what we still don't know about the merfolk.

They've managed to avoid us for so long. And now they're washing up on quiet beach town shores, getting caught up in crab traps, ending up in small creeks like the one behind my home, two hundred miles from the coast. I know it's nothing I did personally, but I feel personally responsible anway.

When Donté leaves I am exhausted from not being pulled under by all that has passed between us unsaid. So I rest, and the merfolk sings me a song while I sleep. I can't say for sure, but I think it has to do with stars, and how different they look from underwater compared to when you finally come up for air.

MONDAY

It's the baby that wakes me. Two swift kicks to the kidney and I'm up. And that's when I register the banging on the front door. My brain conjures up three different worst case-scenarios before my feet even touch the floor.

Surprisingly, Donté was not one of them. Donté's hands are shoved deep in his pockets, his lips pressed together in a thin line while waiting to be let into the house we shared until two weeks ago. His eyes are shadowed and his face stubbled. I was not expecting to see him. Not yet.

His gaze searched my face, glanced over my belly, before landing back at my face. "Why'd you knock?" I ask him.

He shrugged before answering, "I didn't know if you changed the locks and I--" He had to clear the gravel from his throat twice before continuing. . "I didn't want to scare you by just walking in."

"Why are you here?"

But before he can say anything at all sound is pouring out of the master-bath, down the stairs, and pooling around us in the front doorway. It's a last-battle cry, not one that promises victory but ferocity instead. Perhaps my guest is angry at finding itself in a porcelain prison, and it preferred it's murky shallows to this. But I'd like to believe we were connected somehow, even then.

Donté's eyes widen. And he cautiously steps around me into the house. I wait downstairs while he investigates. When he comes back he looks at me without censure. He knows me too well--he knows all the reasons I couldn't leave it there injured, or toss it back or turn it in-- without me saying anything.

Instead he makes a plan and promises to be back tomorrow. You, my child, have been quiet listening to your father's voice. He lingers in the doorway, not looking at me, but at you. Something in me crumbles at the sight. I take Donté's hand and lay it on your back, so he too can feel your soft rolling.

There are tears welling in his eyes.

"I won't keep your child from you, Donté."

"That's not the same as seeing her every day. Growing up in a two-parent household, Lee."

"No it's not. But she'll be loved just the same."

"But--"

"No buts, Donté. You made your choice already."

I can see him swallowing back the arguments he's been practicing in his head. Because I'm right, and he knows it. He says he wasn't thinking straight when he destroyed the only thing I had left of my first pregnancy. That he was lost in a jealous haze of my life, my loves, before him. It doesn't matter though--it was still a choice he made that brought everything crashing down around our heads.

SUNDAY

It must've washed up in the storm. That was my best guess. For four days straight heavy thunderstorms rolled through town. The kind of summer storms that I miss dearly come the muffled quiet of February. The boundaries between Grand Creek and the White Oak Trail are thin here. Once there were swatches of dense shrubs and vegetation as deep as the oaks are tall. These days it doesn't take much before the river swells and takes over, turning the riverbanks into nothing more than a submerged suggestion. Heavy rainfall or snowmelt will send murky water flowing into the meadows on the other side of the trail. It must've washed in with the storm, and got trapped in the shallow valley as the water receded.

It was the lonely keening that caught my attention. High-pitched and frail. As I rounded the corner I realized I was approaching the harrowing sound, and then it was everywhere all at once. My fetus can hear now, though it's usual sounds are my heartbeat echoing through my body. The swishing and susurring that surely must be a part of swish-swaying within someone else. And even if my baby couldn't hear what I was hearing, I bet she could feel it. I certainly could. The strange vocalization surrounded me, reverberated through me.

Then the noise stopped and I spun around trying to figure out where the forsaken sound was coming from. I know despair when I hear it.

And that's when I saw it. A small movement that caught the sun just right. A small blueish glimmer in a muddy puddle of weeds.

I use one of Donté's old fishing nets to free it and try not to wince at what it might look like I'm doing. But the poor thing didn't have much fight left in it; darkness oozed from a wound on its flank. It lifted its head and offered me another one of those soul-piercing wails. This is a song that says 'I have reached my end and there is more I would have done'. It is a song that says, 'I am sick to leave you, will you honour me with your mourning?' And I was in tears before I reached my home. The grief of that last song sat so deeply in my chest that it seemed likely that it'd be all I'd ever feel again.

It didn't feel right doing my night-time routine in the bathroom that the merfolk was recovering in so I move my toiletries to the half-bath. I have a new ritual to end my day with--I got a stethoscope, and now that the baby's heart is big enough, strong enough, I listen to it's tom-tom-tom before I fall asleep.

As I lay in bed, the siren continues its mournful song and I let myself be swept away in it.

In this moment I might not be able to see the path through my grief, but I take comfort in knowing that I am not alone.

About the Author

K.S. Walker is a speculative fiction writer from the Midwest with a fondness for stories with monsters, magic, and/or love gone awry. When not reading or writing you can find them adventuring outside, or inside starting a craft project they may or may not finish. K.S. Walker has previously been published at FIYAH Literary Magazine of Black Speculative Fiction.

Teen Judges' Choice Winner

Chasing Rainbows
Kevina Clear

Up on Aonach Dubh, I felt the freest I had since coming to Glencoe. Down in the glen lay our house and byre, white specks in the dirty valley. A muddy cart-path ran from the barn, curving around the house, over the stone bridge that spanned the River Coe, and out to the drovers' road. To the east, Loch Achtriochtan rippled in the growing wind. A cold gust whipped my skirts and pulled at my hair. From the west, black clouds rolled in over Meall Mor, roaring like hungry beasts.

"Can we go back now, Trissa?" My little brother frowned in worry.

A raindrop hit my forehead, quickly followed by another. "Alright," I sighed. "Let's go."

Hand in hand, John and I scrambled down the mountainside. Raindrops pelted us while the sky overhead grew darker. Lightning flashed. Moments later, the crash of thunder reverberated through the glen.

The house was still so far away. I pulled John into a run. He kept up, though his shorter legs had to work hard to keep up with mine. Then, my foot caught on a rock. I flew through the air and slammed into the ground, shoulder first. Pain jolted through my arm.

"John?" I groaned. "Are you hurt?" No answer came.

"John?"

I sat up, my shoulder screaming with every move. "John?"

A few yards from me, he lay motionless, his head against a boulder. "John?" I whispered.

I awoke, gasping for air, my heart hammering in my chest. The memory of my brother, dead on the mountain, had haunted me for thirteen years, in my dreams and in my waking. No matter how far I went, I could never escape it. Now I was back in Glencoe, the dreams were more vivid than ever.

Through the window of my room in the inn, the crescent moon cast its light onto the floor. I wrapped a cloak around my shoulders and crept down the stairs, through the main room and out the front door. The chilly night air steadied my breathing and calmed my churning stomach. In the distance, Aonach Dubh lay like a sleeping body in the moonlight. I could see why they called it the "Black Ridge."

The first time I saw this valley, I hated it. I'd been raised out on the open moors of Ayr in the south of Scotland, by the sea. In the vastness of land, sea, and sky, I felt small, yet part of everything around me. When the salty wind blew across the water, I imagined I was flying with it, riding free on the back of the breeze. My younger brother John and I would play on the beach or on the heath, running wild until night fell. Those were happy days.

The year I turned eleven, they came to an end.

Da's cousin was clan chief of the MacDonalds in Glencoe, and he needed tenants to farm sheep on his estate. Da, Mum, John, baby Eila, and I said goodbye to our home and left to start a new life in the Highlands. The mountains there were unlike anything I'd ever known. They rose around me like walls, blocking the horizon, cutting off my view of the sky. I had felt like a bird in a box: trapped and afraid, waiting for something terrible to happen.

Not long after we came, it did happen.

I'd been so foolish. I thought if I could climb the mountain and reach its very top, I wouldn't feel so confined. When I told John my plan, he wanted to come. On a bright April morning, we set out to conquer Aonach Dubh. The higher we climbed, the lighter I felt. I was so determined to reach the peak, I ignored the darkness creeping in from the west. John wanted to go back, but I couldn't bear to stop. If I hadn't been so stubborn—if, if, if.

I had been responsible for John. He'd depended on me to take care of him. And I had failed him.

After John died, nothing was ever the same. Da withdrew into himself, shutting me out.

Mum, enveloped in her grief, had room only for little Eila. I'd been left alone.

Thirteen years later, I was still alone. I gazed up at the star-filled sky, the familiar constellations comforting me. They were the same stars that had shone from the beginning of time, and they'd go on shining until time came to its end. I paced outside the inn until the eastern sky lightened to gray.

Before the sun had crested Altnofeadh and dissolved the morning mist, I was on my way back to my old home. I followed the drovers' road through the valley along the river. Cuckoos called to one another, their cries echoing in the stillness of morning. Wispy clouds, pink with the sunrise, danced across the pale blue sky. I pulled my cloak tighter against a sudden biting wind.

The previous day's rain had brought out the wildflowers. Primroses and bluebells peeped their little faces out, bright spots of color in the bareness of mid-April. Bluebells always reminded me of Eila. She was ill often and had to stay in her room. I took bunches of bluebells to her bedside, to give her a bit of the outdoors. When she was well, she loved to pick them herself to bring to Mum and me. Sweet Eila. I missed her.

She'd been ten years old when I'd left, seven years earlier. Even now, I could see her red-rimmed eyes as she begged me to stay. I'd promised to come back one day and take her with me. It tore me to leave her, but I couldn't stay. Not after hearing what Donald told me.

Donald Alastair was a handsome sheep drover who came to drove our sheep to market when I was seventeen. I fell in love at once. He was everything my young heart had dreamed of: tall and dark, with sparkling eyes and a roguish smile.

He saw me in a way no one ever had before. When he looked at me, I felt as if he could see into my soul. While we rounded up the sheep, Donald saw me gazing up to the mountaintops.

He leaned against his staff. "Beautiful, aren't they?"

I shook my head. "Not to me."

"You don't like it here?"

"No." I plucked a piece of grass and tore it into tiny pieces. "This valley feels like a cage to me. I need space to spread my wings."

He shrugged. "You could leave with me."

My heart beat faster. Was he serious? I decided to act as if he were jesting. "And where would we go, Mr. Alastair?"

He gazed off toward Loch Leven. "Well, to start with, we could find the end of the rainbow."

"I like the sound of that. How will we get there?" "We'll build a boat and sail until we reach it."

I sighed. "I do love the sea."

"We'll sail around the world as far as you want." He drew close to me, his face nearly touching mine.

I turned away. "The place I'd really like to go to is home."

"Home?"

"To Ayr. That's where we lived when I was a child. I remember the sky over the sea, nothing but blue."

He took my hand in his. "We'll go to Ayr, then."

The words swirled inside me, whispering in the corners of my heart. It was a beautiful fantasy, and I wanted it to be true.

"I mean it, Trissa. Will you come with me?" His deep blue eyes gazed down at me.

My heart pounded with the idea of leaving. Then I thought of Eila. "I couldn't leave my family. Eila's sick so often that without John, I'm the only one they can rely on."

"John was your brother, is that right?" I swallowed. "Yes."

A breeze rustled through the oak trees. I wanted to tell Donald everything, to empty my chest of the tightness I'd held since that day, that horrible day when my stupidity killed my brother.

He didn't ask me to tell him more. That made me feel I could trust him, that he was safe.

So I told him about coming to Glencoe, about climbing the mountain, and about my enduring guilt.

Donald was silent for several moments. "It makes sense now," he murmured as if to himself.

"What does?"

"Something your father said. He told me about John dying so young, and I said it didn't seem fair. He said not a day goes by that he doesn't curse the one who failed at protecting his son."

I felt like the air had been pushed from my lungs. Da blamed me. I was the one who had failed.

If he cursed me every day, what was the point of being here? It would be better for everyone if I left.

"I'll go."

And I did. Mum and Da tried to stop me, but I was done letting them keep me here, done waiting for love they would never show me. Eila was the only one I regretted leaving.

After Donald and I took the sheep to market, we sailed down the western coast, through the North Channel and into the firth of Clyde, porting at Ayr. When we stepped onto the shore, I waited for the free feeling of my childhood to return, for the heaviness on my heart to lift.

It didn't. I felt the same as I had in Glencoe: trapped

The sea and the sky looked the same as it had when I was young, but I was different. The girl I'd been, carefree and innocent, was gone.

Donald and I traveled together for a time. Before long, I saw a side of him unlike the kind, gentle man who'd said he would take me to the rainbow's end. This new Donald was often angry and shouted at me over nothing. I put up with him until he hit me. Then I left.

Alone, I wandered around the world. I sailed to Ireland, Italy, and India. Though I was freer than I'd ever been, I still felt chained to Glencoe and the past. I longed for love: real, lasting love. The only person who I thought might love me yet was Eila. I imagined her trapped in that cursed valley, and knew I had to return for her.

After seven years, I decided she was old enough to leave. I would show her the world. First, though, I needed to get her out of that valley.

The whitewashed stone house stood at the foot of the mountain, flanked by pine trees on either side. By the shores of Loch Achtriochtan, lambs frisked about while their mothers grazed on the new grass.

I turned off the road onto the path leading to the house. Halfway across the old bridge over the river Coe, I stopped. Water rushed down the river, passing under the bridge on its way to Loch Leven and out to the sea. I wondered if I should follow it, go back to the sea, and forget this place. But I couldn't forget Eila. I'd made a promise, and I would keep it.

Squaring my shoulders, I stepped off the bridge. My boots squelched in the muddy cart- tracks. Through the glen, a lark's song echoed, carried on the breath of the breeze. I caught a whiff of smoke wisping from the chimney. Mum would be cooking breakfast now, while Da finished tending the sheep. And Eila, well, she'd likely be gathering bluebells. What would they say when they saw me? Suddenly, my courage failed me. I wasn't ready. Not yet.

I veered to the right, past the sheep-paddock and around the pine trees. On the other side, I knew, a burn flowed down the mountainside to the river. I could fill my empty water jug there and work up my pluck.

As I rounded the trees, I found I wasn't alone. Several yards upstream, a young woman filled two wooden buckets. Unaware of my presence, she sang softly while she dipped a bucket into the cool, clear water. When she tilted her face toward me, my breath caught in my throat. I knew that face. It had lengthened and matured, but the smile was the same. My baby sister wasn't a baby anymore.

Eila set down the bucket and plucked a bluebell from a clump growing by the water's edge. Her love for them clearly hadn't changed. I watched her as she gathered a rainbow of wildflowers: bluebells in shades of blue and purple, white stars of wood anemone, cheery yellow primroses and celandine, and pink-flowered lousewort. She smiled as she picked the flowers, looking on them as a mother looks on her child.

Her gaze rose to the mountains and the sky, the way mine used to. The difference was that where I'd seen only a mound of stone that stood in my way, she looked on the mountain

with awe and delight. The joy on her face amazed me. She wasn't trapped. She loved this valley like I loved the sea.

"Oh!" She turned and finally noticed me. "Hello there." I smiled. "Hello, Eila."

Her brow furrowed, then relaxed. "Trissa?"

She gasped, then ran to me, her arms wide open.

It felt good to hug her again, though it wasn't like the last time. Her shoulders were level with mine now and she had a strength about her, not like the sickly child I remembered.

I pulled away and looked at her. Her face had broadened and her cheeks glowed. "You've grown up."

Her smile faded. "You've been gone seven years. Did you think I'd still be ten years old?"

I felt rebuked, though her voice held only sadness. "I didn't think I'd be welcome."

She took my hand in hers. "Of course you're welcome. We love you. You know that."

I pulled away. "Do I?"

Tears welled in her eyes. "How can you say that?"

"Well, I can't say you don't. Perhaps even Mum does, in her way. But Da doesn't, not if he curses me every day for not protecting John."

She stepped backward. "Why would you ever think that?"

"It's what he told Donald."

"Donald told you that, and you believed him?"

I shrugged. "Why not? After John died, Da never was the same toward me."

"That doesn't mean he curses you!" Eila's voice broke. "Trissa, I was here, after you ran off. I was here when he went out to the barn thinking no one was there, when he sobbed and pounded the wall with his fist. He told Mum it was bad enough that he'd failed to protect John, but to fail you too... It tore him apart."

Her voice became gravelly. "So don't you go telling me he told that man anything. If he curses anyone, it's himself."

Could it be that Donald had warped the truth so I would leave with him?

There was no doubting Eila's sincerity. If she was telling the truth, that meant Donald had lied to me. He'd promised me freedom, but all he'd given me was chains.

Without realizing it, I smiled.

Eila's tear-stained face twisted in confusion. "Why are you smiling?"

"He lied to me."

"Is that funny?"

"No." It was...freeing. Da didn't hate me. He loved me—he'd tried to protect me from Donald. I could feel the chains breaking, feel the heaviness lift. Growing in my chest, I felt the freedom I thought I'd lost that day up on the mountain.

"Are Mum and Da in the house?" I burst out. "I want to see them."

Her eyes glowed. "Yes, of course."

We each took a bucket and started back to the house. Eila clutched her flowers close to herself. Neither of us spoke.

Eila set her bucket by the kitchen door, and I set mine beside hers. She opened the door and held it for me.

I stepped inside. Da sat at the table, his back to the door.

Mum stirred a pot over the fire. "There you are, Eila—" She looked up and saw me. The spoon she held clattered into the pot.

Da turned around in his chair. His shoulders lifted. "Trissa."

"Hello Da, Mum." I set my pack on the floor.

Mum rushed to me and hugged me. I let myself sink into the warmth of her embrace. Da smiled while a tear rolled down his cheek. He opened his arms to me.

I lay my head on his shoulder and closed my eyes. I was home.

About the Author

Last summer, the seed of this story was planted when Kevina Clear heard "The Whole of the Moon" sung by Celtic Woman. The idea germinated and grew, blossoming into the story you just read. Given her fondness for botanical metaphors, it may come as no surprise to learn that Kevina plans to practice small-scale organic vegetable farming as her profession in the future. For now, Kevina studies chemistry, pre-calculus, — and whatever else captures her imagination — at her home in southwestern Michigan, where she enjoys caring for her family's dairy goats and many gardens, reading, sewing, knitting, and making music with her family.

Teen Judges' Choice Runner-Up

Help Is On the Way
Meghan Hemmer

This story includes references to suicidal ideation. If you are experiencing thoughts of suicide or self-harm, contact the National Suicide Prevention Lifeline at 1-800-273-8255.

A man walked silently along the crowded NYC sidewalk. It was a Friday afternoon, and the hustle and bustle of people anxious to get home to their families was in full force. From above, the sidewalk looked like an ant's nest, and the man easily blended into the crowd; not immediately distinguishable from a distance, or even up close. He wore a frown on his face, the same expression one might make after stepping on a piece of gum, chewed up and discarded on some sidewalk and now stuck to your shoe. His hair was short yet unkempt, sticking up in some places and cascading over his ears, a sharp contrast to the clean-cut tie and suit jacket he wore. Indeed, his wife had ironed them that morning, carefully smoothing out all the wrinkles that had been accrued from the jacket spending the night on the floor; far from its comfortable hanger in the closet. She had sighed as she worked, wondering where her previously well put-together husband had gone, replaced by a man who was distant, quiet, and seemed to lack the energy to do even the most basic of tasks.

His eyes were cast downwards as he shuffled through the crowd taking in the cold, cracked concrete beneath his feet. A storefront caught his eye, the local deli where he had spent many mornings with a cup of coffee and a bagel, reading the newspaper before he headed into the office. He worked on 53rd street, at a small law firm as an accountant. *Worked.* The word stung as it reverberated through his mind and he clutched his briefcase tighter, feeling the unusual weight of various memorabilia crammed inside, remnants of his newly packed up office.

"I'm sorry," his boss had said. "You used to be our best employee. Now, your performance is ineffective to say the least. We can't afford to keep anyone on who is unwilling to work." The man simply stared blankly and said nothing. Although he was not surprised by his dismissal, he was in disbelief nonetheless.

He approached a set of steps. Their stone surface was slightly chipped but otherwise intact. On the sides, ivy covered railings supported planters filled with wilted flowers. A faded welcome mat groaned under the man's feet as he inserted his key into the lock, but instead of entering, he hesitated, taking a quick glance toward the street inspecting the parking slot allocated to his apartment. His wife would not be home from her shift at the nursing home until later that evening, but on rare occasions she would leave work early to relax in the house. Today, the parking slot was empty.

Throwing his briefcase haphazardly on the floor, he plodded into the kitchen. His eyes roaming, the more intimate details of his surroundings stuck out like never before. Swirly lines of marble backsplash layered upon green wallpaper danced before his eyes, causing the man to feel disoriented and nauseous. Green had never been his favorite color, in fact he had adored the brownish color that had previously inhabited the walls. But it didn't matter anymore, of course.

The man blinked, suddenly feeling disoriented and nauseous. Shaking his head, he grabbed a cup and filled it with cold water from the faucet. He took a gulp, feeling the liquid slide down his throat, then dumped the rest in the sink.

Back into the hallway he went, eyes straight ahead, tuning out the frames that layered over the faded wallpaper. The dinner with his wife, his old dog holding a withered stick, his nieces and nephews, all staring down at him. He climbed the wooden stairs, the worn-out floorboards crying out with each painful step. His head throbbed. When he woke up, thoughts had banged against his skull like birds desperate to escape. Now he was numb, but the feeling still lingered.

The man's study was a shabby sort of place. Cleanliness was never the man's strong suit, but an acceptable level of general untidiness had turned into a disorganized mess. Papers littered the desk, floor, and were crammed into bulging file cabinets. Empty mugs of coffee inhabited everywhere papers did not, some having turned on their side dripping onto the already dingy surfaces where they lay. Plaques and diplomas hung on the walls. Once the man had taken pride in polishing them, now a thin sheen of dust cloaked the frames.

Now the man, looking at the grime and mess, sighed and approached his desk, focused on only one drawer. He grabbed the brass knob and pulled it open. The drawer opened easily, the man had opened it many times before and knew its contents by heart. Paper clips on the right, rubber bands the center, post-its the left, and in the back his prized pistol.

His fingers grasped onto the cold medal of his gun, then let go and withdrew from the drawer, shaking slightly. The man felt his chest rise into his throat, choking him from the inside as he firmly held his hands against his body. He could feel his heart beating, faster and faster, like a wild animal was trying to escape his chest.

Outside the small window, billowy clouds had obscured the sun, turning the sky into a dull hue of gray. Seeing this, the man yanked the gun out of the drawer and held it to his head. He squeezed his eyes shut, finger twitching on the trigger. Time seemed to stop, and to the man, everything was deathly still and quiet. Tears had started to roll down his cheeks, dripping onto the floor. The cold metal of the gun throbbed against his temple, his hand shaking and legs like jello. The man thought of his family, his wife and brothers, his parents. He thought of his friends and the man at the deli. Would they miss him?

The question stung as it reverberated throughout his mind and he sank to the floor, dropping the gun as he fell. It clanged as it hit the ground, a sharp metallic sound then the room was silent once more. The man frantically reached into his pocket and dug around until he felt his fingers grasp onto his cell phone. With a shaking hand, he unlocked it and stared at the screen, not quite knowing what to do. His fingers moved on their own and typed "Help me", then pressed search. Clicking on the first number that came up, he listened as it rang, once, twice, three times, then a voice on the other end of the line. He collapsed into sobs, tightly gripping onto the phone. After a few minutes, he composed himself enough to say his name. Then slowly it all came out. The loneliness. The fatigue. The hopelessness. And eventually the gun.

The relief was palpable, it was like a weight had been lifted off his shoulders, the stress of the past months slowly cooling down after being in full force. The tears flowed like a stream, calming the man as they dripped down his cheeks. The man felt nauseous staring at the gun discarded on the floor, and listened to the concerned voice talking to him. The world seemed to spin before his eyes, and the man shuddered as he realized how close he had come to ceasing to exist. How close he had come to no more sunsets and rainy days that end in rainbows. No more coffee at the deli nor kissing his wife when she returned home after a busy day at work. Although the voice had only eased the burden, not removed it from his back, he complied when the voice told him to place the gun back in the drawer then go downstairs.

The man stayed on the phone until he heard the familiar sound of a key turning in the lock, and greeted his wife. At that moment, his wife understood, and rushed to him in concern. The man simply sobbed, and his wife, whispering in his ear, promised him that everything was going to be ok, that help was on the way. And, for the first time in many months, the man believed it.

About the Author

Meghan Hemmer is a junior from Houghton, MI. She enjoys math, playing with her rabbits, and waterskiing. Meghan hopes to major in biomedical engineering in college, and go on to become a reconstructive plastic surgeon. Meghan is very thankful for being chosen to be in the top 10, and hopes this story will spread the message to stop the stigma surrounding mental health.

Teen Readers' Choice Winner
This Chapter of Our Lives
Meredith Mead

The first time I saw her was from a half-off shelf in a bookstore on Elm Street. She was hard to miss. Instead of a coat, she wore a cloak, pinned down to her sides by her backpack, and the top half of her hair was braided back with a flower. There was only one word to describe her—character. Luckily, being one myself, I was an expert on the subject.

I pressed my nose to the inside of our book cover and watched as she perused the shelves, running her hands reverently along the spines. This was no ordinary shopper. This was a girl who lived for words. I could see it all from the thirst in her eyes, the sparkling gleam when she spotted a story that caught her attention. She would lift it hungrily and flip through the pages, only to set it down moments later, searching for the one book that would fulfill her longing. This was the kind of child we dreamed of. She was the one we had been waiting for.

I can't describe how my heart sped up when she stopped in front of us. Erica says I grabbed her hand so hard her fingers nearly snapped, but she's known to exaggerate. (I mean, just look at her plotline) Nevertheless, when this wandering soul leaned down and stroked our book, I knew she was the one, the child we would guide home. Barely daring to breathe, I waited as she picked us up.

"Positions!" I hissed to Erica and any other characters who might be listening. If we were lucky, she'd open to the first page which had about two paragraphs of description before our scene began, just enough time to prepare. If she opened to the middle... she could open anywhere, and we'd have to be ready to improvise. Luckily we knew our story so well, whatever sentence she read, we were ready to act out. I just hoped Cameron, who thought it would be a slow day, hadn't gone back to the museum's treasure corridor; that scene wouldn't come until page 112. Thankfully, luck was in our favor. Opening the cover, the girl tenderly turned to the first page.

I don't remember much about the scenes that followed. My performance was a haze, lost in her rapture and the glowing smile spreading across her face. All I know is that I have never seen a girl and a story so in love. It was as if she was our purpose, and we were her world... until suddenly, it all ended. She was pulled from our realm by a ringing in her pocket. Her head whipped up. She fumbled for her phone, checked the time, and in seconds, streaked out the door. Only when she was halfway into the street did she realize she still held our book. Frenzied, she rushed back inside. Before setting us down, she placed a quick kiss on the cover and whispered a breathless, "I'll come back," before disappearing into the dying November light.

And she did. Every afternoon she returned. She never stayed over an hour, but it was always the highlight of her day, those stolen moments standing in a deserted book aisle. It's hard to say who enjoyed it more, her or us. Little by little, one chapter at a time, she lived our story. The day she turned the final page, it was as if we all let out a collective breath, amazed at the journey we had taken together. She was the best reader we had ever had. Never had I seen such a connection. It was as if we understood everything about each other, and from how she crushed that book to her chest after reading the last word I knew the feeling was mutual. For her, she had found the friends she never had.

Our hearts all broke that night watching her leave. She had found a kindred spirit in all of us. The thought of not seeing her again was...well, as Erica put it, *tragic*. This time, she wasn't exaggerating.

"Hugh," she said as I watched our girl walk out the door. "There's something special about her."

"I know."

Her gaze turned thoughtful. "I wonder what will happen to her. I hope we see her again someday."

I smiled. "Yeah. Me too."

No one could believe it when at the crack of dawn the next day, she walked through the door, a wad of babysitting cash clutched in her hand, plucked our book off the shelf, marched us to the cash register, and walked out of the store with us—without taking a bag. No, she carried us in her arms all the way to the bus stop and then to her first hour. She held us under the desk out of sight and began reading all over again. In third hour, we were confiscated and placed on the teacher's desk until the bell rang. At lunch, a boy from a popular table came over and grabbed at us, leafing through the pages mockingly. As he read sentences out loud, our bodies grudgingly followed his words, but my face was red with anger. How dare he take her book. How dare he poke fun at our girl. I watched through the cover as her cheeks burned, and she snatched us back. Erica remarked that she should have hit him over the head with it, which she was probably close to doing, but sadly she had more common sense than we did. She only sank back into her seat, making sure her hair hid her face as she leaned over the pages so no one could see her eyes welling.

At the end of the day, we were taken home to her small house and even smaller room, placed on a shelf waiting just for us. Then she beamed, and the whole room seemed to glow, and that is how I met Waverly Grace.

She really is a fascinating girl. Unfortunately, I don't think the world is wise enough to see her for what she really is. What any decent character would recognize as kindness, imagination, or brilliance, her peers dismiss as odd. The thought makes my blood boil. I've seen the way she comes home from school, head drooping and eyes hollow. I'm all but ready to draw my sword, slit the cover, and charge into school with her... What would her classmates say then, if we walked in arm and arm? But it doesn't work like that, and no matter how helpless I feel, I can't cross into her world. The cover holds. All I can do is offer her a place to escape when she needs us most.

I like to watch her though. Her room is a pale blue, and she enjoys painting silver stars on her walls. She sits on her bed directly across from our shelf to do homework, pencil behind her ear and a constant grimace on her face. She talks to herself a lot—*It's going to be okay. Just one step at a time, darling, one step at a time*—or she hums bars of songs I've never heard before.

There have been times I swear I heard her mutter snippets of our lines to herself in a voice that doesn't sound like her own— is that how she imagines us sounding?—and I grin.

She cries a lot, too. It breaks my heart every time. One night she brought us to bed with her, her arms curled around the book. I saw the blue of the wall all night long, or if she rolled over, the white ceiling. Occasionally she'll stand in front of our shelf and do nothing more than gaze up at us. If she's feeling especially desperate, she'll hug our book to her chest or talk to us as if we can hear her. She admits to feeling foolish for this, but what she doesn't know is that we're all hanging on every word, cheering her on every step of the way. Her loudest cheers are the ones she can't hear because while we are her lifeline, she is our life.

It's been several years since she took us home. School is no easier, people are no kinder, but we remain her consistency. Today she approaches our shelf, and we all scramble into our positions. She's read us five times already. She could open to any scene, and we'd have to dive right in without a moment to lose. The adrenaline is exciting though. It keeps us on our toes.

She opens to page 237, and I smile. I've always liked this part. I get into stance across from Erica and get ready for my line. (*You're going to pay for this!*) We're not friends yet at this part of the story, but we don't really hate each other, of course. Still, Erica tries to act her part convincingly even though half the time I can tell she's trying not to laugh. By now, we've reenacted these scenes so many times for Waverly, we've grown a bit relaxed, but as clumsy as we can be sometimes, we feed off each other's energy and always manage to make it through. Besides, by now Waverly knows it so well, our performance doesn't really matter. She could recite it herself.

That's the cool thing about readers. They see what they want to. Even if your performance isn't one-hundred-percent accurate, they know what's supposed to happen, so that's what they see. It's like how once they imagine you a certain way, there's no going back. If they imagine you swinging your sword with your left hand, it doesn't matter how many times you deliberately use your right. They'll always remember the left because that's who you are to them. With anyone else it could get frustrating, but with Waverly, it's endearing.

She's in high school now though, and our book isn't exactly cool anymore. In fact, we haven't been officially brought to school since the first day she bought us. Sometimes we'll get a ride in her backpack if it's a rough day. She'll reach inside and brush her fingers along our spine, as if hoping to draw strength from us. *Just step one at a time, darling,* I whisper. *One step at a time.* Just one more hour, one more class, one more day…

Still, when her hand rests on us dejectedly, I long to whisper those words to her in person. I can't, of course. Instead, I have Erica put a hand on the inside of the cover and send her magic into its surface. It makes me feel more in control, and though Erica's healing powers can't travel to Wavely's world, much less heal a broken heart, it always seems to cheer her up, as if somehow she can sense us. If Erica does it long enough, I see her grin, and the hand disappears from the backpack and back to the top of the desk. Then I know we have done our job and can let out the breath I've been holding.

Today though, it's too much. Her trig quiz came back with a D, and a bully slashed her tires the day before the road test. She sits down to do her homework, but it's only moments before she dissolves. With a scream, she hurls her calculator at the wall and sinks to the ground in sobs. I feel my heart constrict as she curls into a ball. She reaches up and yanks the blankets off the bed, burying herself in their fabric. Her cries are muffled, but seeing her lying on the floor sends a new type of rage through me.

I rush for the cover, the barrier between us. I pound my fist against it over and over, desperate to reach her. I can't bear to see her in pain. I need to comfort her, I need to remind her that she is not alone, that the world needs people like her. That she is what makes this room beautiful. That grades are just letters and tires can be replaced. My hand swings… and each time it bounces back. I fall to my knees. If only she knew I was hurting just as much as she was.

I feel Erica's hand on my shoulder. I lower my head, trying to hide my watering eyes. "I can't reach her," I choke. "I can't... I can't help."

She rubs my back gently. "Sometimes we're not meant to help, Hugh. Sometimes we can only watch."

"But someone needs to help her! She's so lonely."

"I know," she whispers.

I bite my lip. *Just send someone to take care of her, I beg. Please. She just needs a friend.*

And then, out of nowhere, it happened. She was sitting in the library, our book hidden beneath her binders when I heard footsteps. They stopped right near us, then a voice said, "Hey. You're Waverly, right?"

This time it was Erica who gripped my hand so hard my fingers nearly snapped. "It's a guy!" she shrieked.

"I just wanted to say, I love your necklace. I noticed it the other day. It's the Silver Falcon, isn't it?"

"Yeah," I heard Waverly say. "They're coming out with a new season in March."

"I know! I'm so excited. I watch it all the time with my brother. What clan would you be in?"

Just like that.

Just as easy as two people meeting in a library. Three weeks later, and they were already official.

"It's what you wanted, right?" Cameron had asked, confused. "For her to be happy?"

Of course it was... just not like this. And yet, I was uncertain whether this really was what I wanted. Now she no longer needed us. It was hard to say I wasn't jealous when she no longer talked to us or took us down from the shelf. With no reader, we were left to ourselves for weeks at a time. Erica took to sulking or running endless sword drills to burn pent up energy; Cameron just haunted the treasure room; I fell into despair. I could only watch, helpless as ever, as everything we experienced, everything we shared together was forgotten.

Until today, their six-month anniversary. I can't take it anymore. We sit around the cover, watching the outside of her empty blue room—she has a movie date tonight.

"I hope they break up," I say at last, shattering the silence. "High school relationships never last, right? Then she'll remember us again."

Erica's eyes widen. "You want him to ditch her? Do you even hear yourself? Look how happy she is. Hugh, you wanted her to find a friend."

"Not a *boyfriend*," I mutter.

"You wanted what's best for Waverly. You can't take it back now just because she doesn't read us everyday."

"But she belonged here! You saw it, Erica, the way she came alive when she was with us.

She was happiest here with us."

Erica's voice turns softer. "You're right. She was made for this world—but she can't live here, no easier than you can live in hers. She has her own life, and she needs to be happy there." She pauses. "Maybe," she says gently, "that was why she found our world. So she can learn to live in her own."

The sound of footsteps in the hall makes me look up. Waverly and Jackson walk through the door. Apparently they're home early. I watch as they sit on the edge of her bed and talk. He makes her laugh, and my heart lifts to see joy on her face. I sigh as guilt washes over me. Yes, I did like being needed, but this, her happiness, is what I want most.

For now, I would have to be willing to fade into the background. She wouldn't always need us. This was just a chapter in our lives, a time we both shared. Soon she would move out, go to college, find a job… she had places to go. The world was waiting for her, they just didn't know it yet. She would leave her mark on this planet, and I couldn't wait to see her do it. And someday, when this world got too stressful, she would return. She would discover us all over again. Until then, I just had to make the most of every moment as our darling, my girl, continued to put one foot in front of the other, one step at a time.

"Oh, Jackson. I've been meaning to share this with you."

I snap out of my thoughts as Waverly stands and walks toward our shelf. I hear Erica gasp. Waverly takes us down and holds us out to him. "This was my favorite book growing up. The characters… I know it sounds crazy, but… they're like family. They got me through some really hard times, and—well—I was wondering if maybe you'd want to read it together."

My jaw drops. We laugh in disbelief. Then everyone's beaming, and Erica's yelling, "places, everyone!" while Jackson flops back onto the bed. Waverly leans on his shoulder. He lifts the book, licks his finger, and flips open to the first page. He begins to describe the cliffs, the castle, the two paragraphs of introduction before our entrance…. I like the way his voice rises and falls. It's soft, but commanding, reassuring in a way that makes you feel safe. *He's a good kid*, I realize. He'll take care of Waverly when I can't. It's this sense that she is in good hands—and us as well, since he literally holds our book—that allows me to slowly let go.

Someday Waverly may think she's forgotten us, but we all know better. She will always come home.

But for now, it's showtime. Even though she can't see, I wink up at Waverly as I take my position. Any moment now. I smile over at Erica. This will be my best performance yet.

About the Author

Meredith Mead is a high school senior from Traverse City, MI. She hopes to attend Cornerstone University to earn a Bachelor's degree in Creative Writing, and she dreams of becoming a young adult or children's book author. When she is not writing, she enjoys spending time with her family, reading books, and going to the beach. Besides being a writer, she is also a singer, a Star Wars fan, and a proud Gryffindor. She would like to thank her friends and family for encouraging her and supporting her dreams.

Teen Published Finalist

˝\drau̇ -niŋ\ (v.)

Dev Buysse

This story includes references to suicidal ideation. If you are experiencing thoughts of suicide or self-harm, contact the National Suicide Prevention Lifeline at 1-800-273-8255.

The water before me is soft. It ripples gently with the breeze that cards cold fingers through my hair and across my bare arms. The sky is reflected plainly on the surface. It is a bright, open thing. The lightness of it is salt in my wounds, but I can't summon the strength of will to be bitter. My seat in the belly of a small boat allows me contact with the freezing water. It shocks the nerves in my fingers, so cold as to be burning. I drag a slow hand through the waves, creating some of my own. They amble away, disappearing silently into the lake. They are of little consequence, in the end, merely a temporary disturbance to a larger body which moves in ways I dare not try to predict. They are small cogs in a colossal system generating something wonderful, and I grieve that I will not be here to see it. There is something there, something beautiful and tragic. A connection tugging at my brain that sits just outside of my reach. I grasp weakly at it, but I am tired, and my soul has long since given up on wanting and curiosity.

My hands work quickly at the rope on the floor, though I do not feel them. There is no sensation of rough fiber scratching along my ankles, no weight to be felt in my hands. Or rather, there is, but no part of me has any need to recognize it. I am detached, a spectator to my body with only mild interest in its movements. The world around me plays in silence, like an old, muted TV delegated to background distraction. A rope ties around legs, the other end attaching to cinder blocks. The boat rocks gently on sapphirine waves, and I am no more than an uncaring observer to my own end.

I stare at the face of the water, the being that would soon claim my life. I stare into it, and someone stares back. They are dead. I see it plainly in their eyes and in the unmoving set of their jaw. As much of a soul lies behind that face as one does behind a mannequin or a wax figure. Less, even, than a painting, for paintings, though inanimate, are the product of care. They are the manifestation of time and emotion. They would not exist had another person not given up a piece of themselves to make it so. They carry a timeless life in them that this empty face in front of me could never hope to match.

Distantly, some part of me recognizes this face. It is one I have seen many times, the same lopsided lips that had sung my favorite songs, the same round cheeks that my mother had held and kissed, the same dead eyes that had met mine in the mirror for as long as I could remember. I know this face, somewhere within me, so why couldn't I name them? They must be someone important to me, though I couldn't ponder who. There aren't many of those left.

Whoever they are, I pity them. They have been sentenced to the same end that I will bring myself to. Nay, I pity the life they had lived, the one we had both lived, to bring us to this end in the first place. I reach out to touch them, and they reach back. Our fingers meet, and their face falls away, swallowed by the endless, rippling maw of waves coming to life beneath my fingers. I wonder, briefly, how that feels. To reach for the surface, for an existence you were told to want but could never truly be grateful for, and be pulled back by the loving arms of the water, by the softness and sweetness of Death. Death would whisper promises in my ear, promises of peace and of silence, and I would know I could trust them. They were the only things I still felt I could trust. I want to reach for that again, and now there is no one to hold me back.

I swing my legs over the side of the boat. My feet dip into the water. Is it cold? Does it hurt? I wish I knew. I wish, faintly, that Death might offer me a few moments of the sensations I've hitherto lacked, before pulling me into his arms. Still, though, I am grateful to him for denying me. This last bit is sure to be unpleasant, and I believe, as does Death, I'm certain, that I have experienced enough unpleasantness thus far. Death is cruel to some, but he is graceful to others, to those that know him and that accept him. As he pulls me into his embrace, my nerves will not sing, and my brain will not cry out, and I will know peace. True, living peace. It is a foreign concept to me. I will be glad to know it in my dying seconds.

I grab at the cinder blocks, but their weight causes my lifeless hands to falter. The skin parts. Blood drips slowly down my palms and it is lovely and terrifying and strange. It is not like the other times I've bled. In the past, when sharp, familiar metal had split my flesh, it had hurt. It had felt like living. The pain had been proof that I was still a breathing, feeling thing. In the past, the blood was warm and came in pulses, the beats of a heart still pumping in my chest. Now, though, I feel nothing. There is no sting of pain or relief, no euphoria, nor even regret. The red spills boringly, no rhythm or dance to it, and there is no warmth. There is none of the heat that is so signature to life. I know for certain, now, deep in my stilling heart, that I am dead. Whether it happened just now, or in a few minutes, or years ago, it matters not.

A thought wanders vaguely in the back of my mind, something about a dead cat in a box, or a silently falling tree. My knowledge of philosophy was once deep and intriguing, but what use has a corpse for the ponderings of the living, for the dynamics of the universe or the complexities of thought?

No, that's wrong. There is purpose to those things, a meaning they might have to the dead. There is amusement. A brief spike of cruel joy at the uselessness of philosophical wondering.

I feel, for the first time in a while, condescension. How stupid I was, for thinking any of it mattered. What fools we all were, for indulging in conclusion-less brain fodder. Where did it ever get us? What point is there in grasping at the inconsequential intricacies of life when it will merely end anyways? Momentary satisfaction? Intellectual superiority? Stupid. Insignificant. Fucking worthless. Why? What was the reason for any of it? What was the purpose of all those years of miserable academia when every ounce of knowledge my pitiful brain has ever amassed will be dead and gone alongside me?

There is a sharp burning in my chest, rising up through my throat. For a moment I think I'm going to retch, but then the heat reaches my head, and I finally recognize it. An old friend, one that had kept me going for years. The burning sensation rings in my skull, thrumming in my ears and clenching my teeth, and it feels like coming home. My protector, my Anger, has returned to see me off. I am grateful for the emotion and the satisfaction it brings me, though that contentment only serves to scare Anger away. Thus is the tragedy of such emotions, I suppose. They love you and care for you when you are at your darkest, but by nature, they cannot be there to see you at your brightest. I grieve it's loss for a moment, welcoming Despair as another beloved acquaintance. She curls up behind my sternum, petting comfort against my ribs. She reaches through my arms, lifting the blocks of cement like I could not, and drops them in the water.

They tug relentlessly at my willing, lifeless body, dragging my corpse into the lake. I sink quickly. Despair slips out and lets me go, placing one final palm to the crown of my head before drifting silently away. For a blissful moment, there is nothing but the heavy water pressing in on all sides. The pressure is deafening, and kind.

As I fall, the currents graze fingers over my clothes and skin, pulling at me to join them. I do so gladly. I watch the surface of the water, watch as the light fades from my vision, hidden by hundreds of gallons of beautiful abyss. When the cinder blocks hit the bottom of the lake, there is nothing but darkness and silence, and I am finally happy. I close my eyes and wait for Death to come for me.

He doesn't leave me waiting long. As his hands pull at mine, my heart hammers to life in my chest. I hear it pounding in my head, a desperate staccato of panic. I had denounced my body so thoroughly, had dismissed it so easily as unimportant, that I had forgotten it could do the same to me. Regardless of my wishes, regardless of my actions, my organs demand I let them continue their tireless work. I had known this would happen, that was what the cinder blocks were for, after all, but it still amused me. That I could be so ready to die, and yet still be in possession of a body that so desperately wants to live, was frankly ridiculous.

Before I can stop it, a laugh bubbles out of my chest at the thought. With it goes the last of my air. It's not long before my lungs begin to throb, though I can barely feel the pain. It is more a background annoyance than a pressing issue. But alas, reflexes are reflexes, and before I can stop it, my mouth opens and I suck in a breath. I fill with water, the new weight of it sinking me down further. I kneel at the bottom of the lake, a congregant to the holiness of the drowned. My lungs have realized they will never see air again, and have ceased their bothersome whining. My heart slows to nothing and my muscles give out. Death wraps his arms around me. My vision fades and my mind goes finally, mercifully numb, and I am free.

About the Author

Dev Buysse is a young author from Caledonia, MI. They have been interested in reading and writing for most of their life. They write mostly fantasy, with some dabbling in poetry. They have hopes of becoming a published author within the next few years. This is their first writing contest, as well as the first work they've shared publicly.

Teen Published Finalist
Fate of the Fallen
Paige Harry

Even the stars were denied recognition until the last rays of a dying sun had surrendered to the night. That could very well explain why it had taken her so long to see the lonely flickering of the lights that hung deadly from the empty store windows. The bells atop the door announced her arrival obnoxiously, blowing what little cover she had. Nimble fingers wrapped tightly around the handle of a curved blade. Her knuckles bulged against her tightly wound skin, turning them a ghostly white. Inside, the checkered tile floors were caked with filth. Tall metal shelves, miraculously stocked full of snacks and sweets, were coated in the blanket of dust that lay undisturbed over it all.

She wasted no time in shoving handfuls of canned fruit, jerky, and whatever else she could find roughly in her bag. There was something about the stillness in the air that made her uneasy. The hair on the back of her neck rose alertly. Blood thundered in her ears. She kept her hand on the blade, ready to strike at a moment's notice. A deafening clatter to her right caught her attention for a moment. One moment too long. Her neck snapped roughly to the side, but it was too quick. A groan of pain escaped her lips as the fier came barreling into her. She struck out blindly. Flesh and steel collided, eliciting an anguished screech from the gut of her victim. She pulled the blade out of the torso where it had originally landed and reared backwards, slamming the blade into its face. It's body crumbled as it fell like a ragdoll to the floor.

Even a moment of hesitation was fatal with these things. The abilities they possessed… no one was safe. The last thing she needed was to have them toy with her mind.

The hiss of hastened footfalls sounded against the hard floor as another came at her. She disarmed the first with lethal precision. Another. She brought her knife down hard against it's vulnerable, unprotected neck. The faulty lights in the ceiling glinted off of the steel in her hand.

A third rushed at her, replacing the blood in her veins with cold dread. Something was off. A veil of darkness followed them wherever they went. A blanket of ash. The face was eerily familiar… almost human… They weren't quite dead, but they weren't exactly alive either. Decay gnawed grossly against its delicate skin. Filth plastered it's hair firmly against the sagging skin of it's hollow face. The putrid stench of blood and decay wafted from the entirety of it's being.

The fier seized it's opportunity in her momentary distraction. The world parted in a vicious scar before her, leaving her staring into the eternal abyss of nothingness that had come to claim her. The atmosphere pulsed with the promise of violence. Winds stirred with a lethal grace. Waves of tar and ash littered in the breeze overcame her. Songs of sirens past nipped at her ears. It was her.

"Cassie..." The siren whispered. "Cassie." it said, louder this time. A cold shiver drove a phantom of a talon down each vertebrae in her protruding spine, leaving her slick with sweat. "Cassie help me!" It shouted at her. "HELP ME!" *It's not real...* She clawed at her ears, trying desperately to escape. The terror inside of her threatened to spill out, leaving her jaw slackened in a silent scream. *It's not real.* It didn't matter though. Her heart beat it's fists rapidly against the sides of it's hollow cage, screaming to be released. The blood in her veins went leaden, leaving her arms heavy and numb at her sides. Her eyes squeezed shut as the voice continued to taunt her.

A pair of cold hands closed around her throat. It was no secret what came next. Fiers trapped their prey with these mind games. They stimulated the part of the brain that processed your darkest fears... and made them come to life. The phantom fingers wrapped tighter around her throat, leaving her lungs begging desperately for the one thing she could not provide them with. It was strangling her. As if the hallucinations weren't enough. Veins pressed tightly inside her eyes, threatening to burst. They bulged as more pressure was placed against her throat. Memories of the past swam in her mind as shadows began to dance softly in the corners of her eyes. Memories of a time when she was happy. Memories of betrayal. Memories of the blood that stained her hands. She shuddered at the thought. Perhaps the past was better off forgotten.

The sound of a gunshot rang between her ears. Vaguely distant, yet vaguely familiar. The blackness around her faded into the air. When the shadows had cleared completely, she could just make out the lifeless body of the fier sprawled across the floor beside her, it's limbs splayed out in awkward angles. Black blood gushed from the gaping hole left by the bullet lodged in its skull. Disorientation was beginning to set in. Spots danced in her vision. Someone stood over her, their lips were moving, but she couldn't make out the words. Panic settled in her chest once again as she began to gasp for air, a hand resting gently over her damaged neck. The face above her began to focus, and words began to form between their parted lips.

"Hey." The voice said, "Hey, are you ok?"

Tall and lean. Clothed in a faded green jacket, tattered undershirt and long cargo pants. A boy. Waves of golden hair tickled the bridge of his nose, shielding his widened eyes.

"Hello?" He repeated, "You good?"

Is he serious? She thought to herself, trying to retain any shred of dignity she had left. "Uh... yeah. I thoroughly enjoy near death experiences, it's a crucial part of my self care routine." She uttered sarcastically. So much for dignity.

She soaked in the dulcet sound of his laugh. It was nice to hear someone laugh. It had been a while. He offered her a hand. She eyed him suspiciously before accepting it.

"I suppose I should thank you." She said, wiping the dirt off of her pants. "That would be the polite thing to do."

Their eyes met for a moment as they took each other in.

"Ok" she said, breaking the eye contact, "well this was fun, we should really do it again sometime." She collected her things before making her way towards the door. Socializing wasn't really her thing.

"So that's it?" He asked from behind her.

"What?"

"Just gonna let me save your life and then take off?"

"Yep."

"Ok" he shrugged. "'Just thought that two people might be better than one right now."

"What do you propose?"

"Come with me. Or let me come with you. You have good instincts, but I know better than anyone how hard it is to be alone out there."

She stopped and thought for a moment. He was right of course, the more allies you had the better, but truth be told she was more of a loner. Had been for quite some time now.

"No."

"Please?"

"Mmm..." she groaned. " Fine."

He beamed at her, his curly hair bouncing over his forehead. If she needed to get rid of him later, she would.

"Great," he said, "but if we're going to do this, you've got to at least give me a name." She whirled back around as she pushed the door open and said:

"Cassidy."

She heard him shuffling behind her to catch up, and he offered her his hand.

"I'm Atlas."

She looked at his hand for a moment, but decided to ignore it.

"Harsh" he said, trailing behind her once more. "So where exactly are we going?"

"Well," she started. " We have weapons. We have food. We have water. I passed a trailer on the way here, seemed abandoned, like everything else. I was thinking it might not be a bad place to hole up for the night."

"Ok."

It had been almost two weeks since the incident at the party store. They had wandered aimlessly and eventually found the old trailer to make camp in. As much as she didn't want to admit it, she was starting to like having a companion. She had forgotten what it was like to not be alone. Though she would never tell Atlas that.

"So is that your real name?" She asked, completely unprovoked.

"What?"

"Atlas. Is that your real name?"

"Oh" he laughed "No. When my family-- when the outbreak happened, it was just too painful. So I changed it."

She nodded her head grimly to show that she had understood. "What was it?"

He shot her a quirky smile. "Jaxon."

"Phew, good thing you changed it." She said jokingly, blowing out a breath. He punched her lightly in the arm, a fake pout on his face.

" I should have left you back there for the fiers!"

They laughed good-humoredly, something they didn't get too often in this bitter life of theirs. The corners of her lips tugged upward in an immovable grin. She gazed at him fondly, tears collected in her eyes from laughing. It seemed as if finally things were starting to look up. She could only hope she wasn't making a grave mistake.

She stood up abruptly, busying herself with tidying up her backpack. In truth her bag was fine, she just needed to distance herself from Atlas. She couldn't risk it. Not again.

The sun rained handcrafted daggers down upon them, leaving their skin raw and red from the heat exposure. They lounged lazily against the side of the peeling camper, desperately clinging to any bit of shade they could find. The two had busied themselves in making a feast of chips from the party store and canteens of water.

"There's been word," Atlas began slowly, popping open yet another bag of chips. "that the fiers were engineered."

"You think the outbreak was … intentional?"

"I don't know for sure, but there's word that a man named Harrison Dilloway, the head scientist at a place called NEBULA labs, had been experimenting on people. And funnily enough, the first fier came from there."

"It's not too far from here," he shoved another handful of chips in his mouth before continuing. "Probably about ten miles east." He said with a crunch, motioning with a finger in the direction they would have to go.

"And where did you hear that?"

"I have a friend in Salus. It's a small city about thirty miles north."

She said nothing. Kept her gaze fixed on something far in the distance. She was more than familiar with the NEBULA project , and she knew Harrison Dilloway all too well. Going there was a death trap, but telling Atlas what she knew could be a grave mistake.

"Even if it started there, even if it was all intentional, what do you think we're going to find?"

He was quiet for a moment. " I don't know. But for once in my miserable existence, I have hope. Hope that maybe, just maybe, there's a solution. And I know, this will probably be a bust, but shouldn't we at least try?"

Another pause.

"So you want us to trek ten miles across an open desert filled with crazed, neurologically impaired lab rats who want nothing more than to tear us apart limb by limb to find an abandoned laboratory where we will likely find nothing of use?"

"That's what I'm saying"

She took a swig of water before saying, "Alright hotshot, I'm in."

The sun had long since been swallowed into the night of the blackened sky. Gusts of frosted wind nipped ruthlessly at her skin, leaving her nose a deep shade of crimson. The cold was brutal, but a fire was too risky. She picked up a scratchy wool blanket they had found on one of their scavenges and draped it over her shoulders. Her feet dangled precariously over the edge of the cliff on which they had made camp. Below her swarmed hundreds, thousands, of fiers scrambling across the dead earth. A voice behind her cut through the tension in the air. Atlas walked up behind her, wrapped in a blanket similar to hers.

"Couldn't sleep?" He asked.

"Haven't tried."

"Yeah me neither."

He found a seat beside her and they sat in silence, taking in the battlefield they would have to cross come morning. His presence put a much needed silence in her mind, saving her from herself.

"Since we're probably going to die tomorrow, I've gotta know;" he paused. "What do you see?"

She hesitated for a moment. She knew exactly what he was asking, but she wasn't sure she wanted to answer.

He laughed lightly, "If I had a run in with a fier, I'd probably see you to be honest. You're quite terrifying."

She sucked in a breath, and shot him a glare. She wasn't prepared to have this conversation. With anyone.

"Existence is a fragile thing." She started, not looking up. "Once upon a time I was in love. And I made a mistake. Trusted someone I shouldn't have. That mistake cost her her life. I see her die every day. Replaying over and over in my mind. I don't think it will ever really go away. Since then I just decided it's better for me to go off on my own. That way the only person I will ever hurt is myself."

They sat in silence again. "What was her name?"

The word stuck in her throat. Her cheeks flushed and tears threatened to spill from her eyes.

"Sam."

Silence.

"It's all his fault." She said quietly. "Those labs? That- that god awful place we're storming into tomorrow? They killed her." She paused for a moment, her head hanging low before choking out, "I killed her."

She stared blankly upward at the brilliant luster of sorrow in the sky.

"Cass, I don't know what happened. I don't know how you were involved with NEBULA. However, I can tell that you loved her, and you would never have intentionally hurt her."

" I did." The emotions became overwhelming and the tears began to fall. " I loved her so much. She was beautiful. Kind. Funny. I never deserved her." She hid her face behind her hands, shielding herself from the world that had taken so much from her.

The decision was made before she had time to think about the consequences. It didn't feel right to hold it in any longer than she already had.

"I worked for him." She said quietly. "Harrison Dilloway." She didn't dare look up. "I worked with him. I helped him start project NEBULA. We were partners. It started as a way to neurologically alter the functions of the brain from the inside. I was a neuropsychologist, so I saw a lot of sick people. I just wanted to find a cure. He had been testing on people behind my back for months. I tried to exploit him... and that's when Sam got involved. His own sister." She shook her head, tears flowing steadily again.

"His... sister?" Atlas asked, his eyes widening.

She nodded her head grimly. "*A group of my own friends* restrained me while he fastened her into the operating chair and made me watch as he cut her open." She paused. "It wasn't long after the procedure that she got sick. I managed to get us out. We got as far away as we could.

But by the third day she wasn't even herself anymore. Violent. Aggressive. Her hair was falling out. Her skin was just barely clinging to her face. She begged me to end it. I didn't have a choice. I- I didn't want to-- she--"

Cloth brushed against the log underneath her as Atlas shifted closer to her. She didn't pull away when he wrapped his arms around her and pulled her closer to his chest. It had been so long since she had felt the touch of another person. Tears tore at the corners of her eyes as she started to cry harder into his shirt. She didn't want him to let go. She was so grateful for that fragment of a friend.

He remained quiet for some time before finally breaking the silence. "Hey Cass?"

"Yeah?"

"We're in this together now. I'm not going to let anything happen to you. Or me, for that matter. Ok?"

"Hey Atlas?"

"Yeah?"

"Thank you."

At last she looked up at him, gazing into his eyes. Pools of warm honey, dancing softly on a bed of copper and chamomile. The cool dampness of a pine forest after a long rain. They were beautiful. She hadn't noticed. She reached out to rest her hand against his cheek. Bits of stray stubble poked at her hand. She was in no business to deny herself the little things in life anymore. She was probably going to die tomorrow anyway. He met her gaze, a perplexing thought swimming soberly behind the quiet contemplation in his softened eyes. Her lips brushed softly against his cheek before she got to work on sharpening her knife, misleadingly calm for the fire that pulsed inside of her. The restless apprehension of dawn crawled across her skin.

The stars would quake underneath a forgotten sun and leave her alone in their ashen dust, for they had taken everything from her. She knew now if anything were to happen to him, her heart would never again be whole. She was going to keep Atlas alive. Even if that meant giving her own life. Fate had tried to leave her bloody, beaten, and bruised. A girl of broken hopes and teardrops lost in the ashes of who she once was. Fate had left her to rot in her own benevolence. By god she would defy it, and by her own name she would reclaim the justice that was rightfully hers.

Harrison, she thought to herself, *I'm coming for you.*

About the Author

Paige Harry is an aspiring author whose keen eye for the realm of fantasy is both a blessing and a curse. She has always been fascinated by the innate ability to create a world that no one else could ever imagine, which often leads to her daydreaming instead of doing her schoolwork... guilty. She is fluent in the art of sarcasm and wit, has an entirely overactive imagination, and an acute sense for making intriguing characters with questionable decision making skills. She is currently working on mastering the art of storytelling so others may enjoy reading her works as much as she enjoys writing them.

Teen Published Finalist

October 8, 1983

Payton Kalsbeek

October 8, 1983, 8:00 pm:
The bustling streets of New York City overflowed, as busy residents continued on nonchalantly, unaware of their futures. Martin Mills sat on his sofa, with the old springs creaky and poking as he plopped down. The floor boards groaned and creaked as his body weight pushed onto the furniture. The stream of conversations and people outside his window clattered his brain and caused him anger at their voices. Martin used to enjoy hearing the voices of others, being a social butterfly, making friends everywhere he went, going to his boring job with excitement just to see his coworkers. That is, until his father's unexpected death. Well, unexpected to everyone but Martin. He came into custody with a pair of glasses just two days before his father's passing. He couldn't quite remember how he came to possess these glasses, especially since his vision seemed quite extraordinary. He shared his father's piercing green eyes that never needed any corrective lenses. But these weren't ordinary glasses, for when the user looked through the lenses, the date and time of death of anyone seen through them appeared above their heads. For this reason Martin knew of his father's death two days before it happened, but did nothing to stop it. There was nothing that could be done.

October 8, 1983, 8:01 pm:
Sitting on the couch, Martin opened his newspaper, once again reminded of the date - exactly one year after his father's death. The guilt, the feeling that filled his whole being everyday, struck a thousand times harder on this day - October 8. All he could do was see and think of the memories of his father, trapped in the glass of wooden squares hanging on his walls, sitting on his tables, and resting on shelves around the whole apartment.

October 8, 1983, 8:12 pm:
After a little more self torture, Martin finally got up to feed what little appetite remained in him. He headed towards his cookie "jar." This jar hardly looked like a jar at all. His father formed it in a pottery class, and

it just looked like a pile of clay, with a hole in it, and a blob for the lid. But a reminder of that caused him to put his hand in to check anyways. The absence of the sweet, chocolaty smell immediately confirmed that the cookies never existed. But this was good. He didn't deserve cookies. His hand remained in the jar, and a large, defeated sigh escaped his mouth. Then his hand touched an object in the empty void. The glasses.

October 8, 1983, 8:13 pm:
Martin pulled the glasses out of the "jar", and turned them over in his hand. He hadn't seen them since he chucked them in there the second his father's eyes closed for the last time. The second he couldn't do anything for him, the second Martin realised his father, everyone he had ever met, and himself, all bore future death. And Martin could tell exactly when that death would take place. This all consuming darkness acted as a thick wall between himself and his father, and would eventually become a wall between himself and his life. He couldn't escape it. No one could. Martin couldn't tell if that darkness of death took the spot of the twisting knot inside of him, or if it was the guilt of that day he expected his father to leave and never return - and he did nothing. But he knew one thing for sure: he feared it.

October 8, 1983, 8:15 pm:
At this point, Martin's pain surpassed his judgement. He needed a connection, a reminder of his father. Pictures were ordinary; everyone had pictures. No one else possessed the glasses.
Martin slowly unfolded the wiry frames, closed his eyes, and set them onto his nose. He deserved these treacherous devices. He opened his eyes to see his same apartment, old and rundown, bones creaking at any movement. It looked the same. What didn't look the same was the street below. The streets of New York City always flooded with people, that remained the same. But those floating dates above their heads haunted Martin to the core.

October 8, 1983, 8:17 pm:
Each person, old and young, shared those numbers mocking them with each step they took, as they continued to breathe, speak, and live. Martin could see each one. Each one he could look at but do nothing to stop. Each one he saw reminded him of his father, weak and pale on his bed, but still smiling at just Martin's presence.

October 8, 1983, 8:21 pm:

One woman, particularly beautiful, strolled down the street, reading the newspaper. So young and pretty, she certainly failed to expect her death in five days. A child, only about seven, skipped down the street with his mother, 82 years left to go. An old man cutting a young man's hair in the barbershop across the street still carried nine more years, while the younger only six. It was funny how it worked that way. Some people seemed more ready than others, but their time to go seemed far later.

October 8, 1983, 8:42 pm:

At this point, over 200 people crossed down just his street with a death date above their heads. Martin felt the grief of each one as he imagined their passing.

October 8, 1983, 8:54 pm:

Martin couldn't do this to himself anymore. Each passing soul, unaware of their fate, tore at him as he sat idly by, unable to save them. They would all die and so would he. He looked away towards the chipping paint of the window sill. His thin finger ran along the cracks, soaking in all the memories of just this window alone. He and his father used to peer through this glass, their clothes getting snagged on the rugged edges, and tell stories as they watched the snow fall in the winter. Just another reminder of what he had lost.

October 8, 1983, 8:55 pm:

Martin slumped down the hallway, feet heavy with despair and fear. Creak. Another sound of his home. The one his father raised him in, and loved for its "rustic class". Its walls depicted Martin's many great years, along with his father's, and his father's, until four generations of images graced the walls. Those old, broken walls. Each brush of wind shook the whole building, like a dead tree in a storm. Creak. Thumps upstairs shook the ceiling, leaving pieces of plaster to flake from the sky. The building, weathered and broken, barely held onto the little support left in it.

October 8, 1983, 8:57 pm:

Creak. Martin's teary eyes grazed the images on the walls, until they stopped on his reflection in the large, circular mirror his father had bought from a pawn shop. Creak. Martin glanced over his ghostly appearance as his eyes were locked on the one thing that could end his suffering: the floating characters above his head - October 8, 1983, 9:00 pm.

October 8, 1983, 8:58 pm:

Creak. Martin hadn't stopped thinking about his father, until now. Now he could only think of his own imminent death. Creak. He was going to leave this world and never return, saying goodbye to anyone he ever knew. Those he saw on the street who would eventually die. Those who visited his father as he was sick and about to die. Creak. Those who visited him after he died. Those who Martin grew up with as a child, who could have already died, but he never knew. Creak.

October 8, 1983, 8:59 pm:

 All these feelings of longing for those he lost, and the fear of being lost, hammered at his brain. Creak. Then a realisation slammed into him, more powerful than any thought he ever had. Creak. He could leave, and be with his father again. Creak. He could leave, and be out of his misery. Creak. The loss and longing weighing him down would vanish and he could be at peace. Creak. Martin looked back into the mirror at the numbers reflecting above his head, closed his eyes, and smiled.

October 8, 1983, 9:00 pm:

Crash.

About the Author

Payton Kalsbeek is a sophomore from Grand Rapids, MI. She's the oldest of 3 children. In her free time, she enjoys painting and drawing, and her favorite media is acrylic paint. She also likes to go camping and going to the beach, and spending time with friends and family.

Judges' Choice Youth Winner

The Adventure Behind the Canvas
Amelia Veltman

"Ugh!" Amy exclaimed. She was in her room, trying to write a story like the famous author Beverly Cleary. Amy had heard about her from her history teacher and had checked out a book from the library that she had written. She was inspired. She got down to work and crafted her story until 12:00 am. Suddenly she remembered that she had school the next day. Packing up her bag for the next morning, thoughts of her story still danced in the back of her mind. As her head hit the pillow, she drifted to sleep, anxious to work on her story again the next day.

When she got to school, she noticed two girls snickering and pointing at a boy. He wore a button-down shirt and jeans and Amy realized that she hadn't remembered seeing him before. He was new to the school. His locker was next to hers, so she figured she would talk to him. "Hi," Amy said, "What's your name?"

"I'm Sam," said the new kid pushing up his glasses. "I'm Amy," she replied. "What class do you have first?" asked Amy.

"History," said Sam.

"Me too!" Amy exclaimed. "I'll show you the way."

Later, at lunch, Amy asked if Sam would sit with her. They talked about their interests. Amy confided in Sam, "I've been trying to write a story, but can't get the words right."

Sam brightened. "Well, if you want help, we could work on it after school. I love writing stories," he said.

"Sure! I'd love some help!" Amy replied.

After school, they went to Amy's house to work on the story. Sam told her about "the Other Side of the Canvas."

"It's a wonderful place, where paintings come alive and unusual characters can speak," Sam's excitement intensified. "Tales become truth and the experience is beyond your wildest imagination! I have been there many times before."

When Sam had finished, Amy exclaimed, "That sounds awesome! I wish I could go there, to learn about storytelling."

"I could take you there if you wanted," responded Sam. "All you have to do is touch a magical, blue medallion."

"Do you have it with you?"

"Yup! Let's go!"

Sam carefully took the pendant out of his pocket, and they walked to Amy's self-portrait that was hanging on her wall in her bedroom. They touched the pendant, and touched the picture, and Amy's room flashed before their eyes. They closed their eyes because of the brightness that surrounded them. When they opened their eyes, they saw they weren't in Amy's room anymore, they were in the drawing. But now it looked different. Suddenly, Amy realized why. It was staring at them!

"Where did you come from?" The Self Portrait sought.

"The other side," explained Sam.

"Well, it's nice to see you again Sam."

"Do you know that painting?" asked Amy.

Sam nodded. He had been to the other side many times before. Amy could see it in the gleam of his eyes, the way he smiled, and the look on his face. But there was a different expression there too, a touch of sadness, something she couldn't quite make out.

"Well, we should probably get going. Lots of stuff to do," Amy stated hurriedly, trying to get the sad expression off of his face.

Instantly, it disappeared. "Yes, we probably should. Thank you for your time, Self Portrait."

"Thank you," responded the drawing.

"This way," Sam gestured toward a hole in the side of the painting that she hadn't noticed before. When they stepped in, the Self Portrait disappeared.

"Come again soon!" Its faint voice exclaimed.

Then, they could see a different painting. Amy recognized it as the painting in her grandparents house. The sky was bright blue, and the trees and grass were a vibrant green. The people were all dressed like fancy, rich aristocrats. There was one thing that really stood out, though. There was a flamingo in a velvet suit with a top hat.

The flamingo walked up to them and said, "Hello, I am Anthony, how may I assist you?"

"Hello, Anthony, I've brought a friend whose name is Amy," explained Sam.

"Oh! Sam, it's you! I trust you have been good, have you?" Anthony asked.

"I've been fine, thank you for asking. We were hoping you knew the way to him," explained Sam.

"Who's him?" asked Amy.

Sam didn't answer.

"To know the path, the way to truth, you must be quick, keen, and stealthy as a sleuth. A very tiring treacherous path it is, with menacing mountains, and deadly cliffs. It is I who will show you the way, through the dangerous valleys cold and gray," Anthony explained. "But to go on this journey, you will have a debt you must pay. To show me the way, to the other side of the painting by the end of the day."

"We can show you," said Sam.

"Well then, let us be on our way," declared Anthony.

So, they went through the painting's hole, which apparently every one had. They ended up in a painting of a grey valley that looked as though it had been deserted for years. Old tents and bones were scattered everywhere. Remnants of the animals presumably eaten by the people that had lived there. They cautiously walked through the valley, watching for anything alive. After they had passed through,they quickly hurried into the hole at the end of that painting. They entered into a different painting that appeared to be a Japanese village filled with people. They walked through the village and Anthony walked up to a booth and asked, "Hello, fair lad. I don't mean to sound mad. See these two and I, we are in some trouble. Is Maxwell here, now on the double?"

So the man ducked back behind the curtain, and out came... a poodle! He wore a Japanese, blue, silk robe, and had many rings. "Hello Anthony, Sam, how may I assist you?" asked the poodle.

"Well," Sam explained, "We need to..." and then lowered his voice to a whisper so low, Amy couldn't hear him.

Maxwell nodded. "Fair enough," he said. "Right this way."

Maxwell led them to a building, knocked on the door, and waited. Finally a soldier opened the door, and when he saw Maxwell, led them in. The soldier brought them to a small dark room. In the room was an old cat in a red robe. Next to the cat was a boiling, steaming basin of a substance that seemed to be whispering words like "perplexing", "incomprehensible", and "inexplicable."

"Hello," said the cat, without opening its eyes. "What brings you before me today?"

Anthony explained that Amy wanted to learn how to storytell so she could write her own story. The cat walked over to a table filled with old charms and books. He picked up the one book that stood out from the rest. He opened it gently and explained, "Storytelling is not an action, but a feeling. A feeling that begins deep inside the soul and grows outwards. It captures your whole body in the glamorous feeling of the tale. You feel a deep connection running through your bones, like you have become one with the story. You can not simply write down the components of the story, but rather experience the characters and become one with them. It is not just spoken, it is grasped by the listener."

The cat handed the book he was holding to Amy and said, "travel through the depths of your soul. Search for the story within you. Use this as your guide. Be well, my friend." And with that, the cat turned and stepped into the boiling, whispering substance they first saw him by, and he was gone.

Amy stared at the book she was holding in disbelief. She turned to Sam and said, "We have a story to write!"

The guard led them out of the building and Maxwell bid his adieu. "I must go back," he said. "I hope this helped.I look forward to reading, upon your return, the outstanding story you will write from this experience."

Sam, Anthony, and Amy walked through the portal in a nearby booth and found themselves in the grey valley they had traveled through to get to the village. They crossed the valley and stepped into the portal that led to the painting in her grandparents house.

Once in that colorful painting, Sam said "there is one debt I have still to pay. Anthony, would you like to travel back with us? A talking flamingo in a top hat and velvet suit would stand out in our world, but a promise is a promise and a debt must be paid."

"May I say my last goodbyes first?" Anthony asked.

"Of course," Amy replied.

Once he had finished his parting words, they were on their way.

They traveled back through the portal that led to Amy's self portrait and through its portal, landing in Amy's bedroom.

"You need a disguise," Sam said.

"Ooh! I know what he could wear!" Amy exclaimed, running to her closet. "I have this awesome Halloween costume that would fit you perfectly!" She pulled a large green and tan lump out of a tote on the floor. Then, she held it up, and they could see that it was a dinosaur. It had a contraption on the back side that blew air into it, so that it would stay blown up.

"It's perfect! Now how do I get in?" Anthony asked.

"Well," Amy explained, "You put your foot in here... Yup! Now the other one... Good! Okay, now put your wings in these holes, and pull this over your head... There! Tada!"

Anthony turned around, but he didn't look like Anthony anymore. He was a dinosaur! "How do I look?" He asked.

"Like a dinosaur!" Sam replied. "You were right, Amy! It is perfect!"

"Amy! Dinner!" Amy's mom called from down the stairs.

"Oh, no!" Amy cried, "I almost forgot! Do you guys want to stay for dinner?"

"Sure!" Sam replied, "And Anthony can sleep at my house. My parents go to the other side a lot, so they won't mind. Then, tomorrow, we can work on the story."

So, they went downstairs and ate dinner and later Sam and Anthony went home.

The next day, they wrote the story. They sent it to a publisher, who released it into stores and bookshops. It was a hit! And to this day, Amy continues to write stories using the methods of the old cat. In fact, the one that you just read was one of them.

About the Author

Amelia is a 5th grade homeschool student who has a flair for drama. She loves to be creative in all that she does. Her favorite pastime is reading books. When the opportunity came up to participate in the Write Michigan contest, she jumped on it. She is creative, compassionate, and has a love for life. She hopes you love her story!

Youth Judges' Choice Runner-Up

The Unexpected Catastrophe

Elle Einfeld

I knew, from the moment that our fifth grade class stepped onto that trail, that I should never have agreed to come. My parents didn't listen, though. They made me come on this wretched school backpacking trip. I even told Jo, and Ms. Lewis. They both disagreed with my opinion. Jo was the type of girl that absolutely *loved* the outdoors. So was Ms. Lewis.

It wasn't like I hated the outdoors. The one and only reason I didn't want to go was that I would be away from my parents. The thought of it churned my empty stomach. I hadn't eaten lunch. Or breakfast. And I had absolutely no intention whatsoever of eating dinner, either.

The last few months, my parents said, "stay home, it's safe. Stay home, it's safe!" Now, they're telling me to get out there and do stuff. They want me to be with friends.

The sound of roaring water filled the air, disrupting my train of thought. A waterfall. I looked up from my shoes. Lush greenery surrounded the waterfall. I looked out across the water on the hilltop observation deck, without actually seeing anything. It would have been breathtaking, if my parents were here. It could not drown out the sound of my heartbeat, getting faster all the while. What if I threw up? My parents would not be there to comfort me. What if I passed out? What if I drowned? What if, what if, what if. All I wanted to do was bury myself in a quiet, peaceful corner of my mind, where nothing existed. Absolutely nothing.

I felt a sharp tap on my shoulder. It was Jo.

"Let's go put our feet in the water!" she yelled, motioning me to follow.

I looked at the group of parents who volunteered, wishing mine were there. It took all my strength to turn and follow Jo, who was already running down the path, her tangled red hair flying out from behind her.

At the bottom of the hill, some adults were already pitching tents. Others were cooking dinner. Just smelling the food made a fresh wave of nausea crash over me. I let the feeling sink in, hoping that if I did, Ms. Lewis would call my parents and they would come and take me home.

"Dinner!" Ms. Lewis called.

All my classmates hurried to the logs that were set out around the fire pit so that everyone could sit down and eat. They sat, chattering, laughing, and spooning giant spoonfuls of the backpacking lasagna into their mouths. It didn't help either that Jo was sitting right next to me, eating noisily.

I closed my eyes, but it didn't help.

"Do you want some dinner?" Ms. Lewis came up behind me. I shook my head. "Alright, but if you get hungry, just come and let me know, okay?"

I nodded, too afraid to speak. She walked back to her own dinner.

"Are you going to eat?" Jo stopped munching to talk. I shrugged. She returned to her eating, but I could see the worry in her eyes. I focused on the flames in the fire pit. It was getting dark.

At about nine o'clock, Ms. Lewis stood up to address my class. My heart started beating even faster. What if a bear came in the middle of the night and gobbled me up? What if I didn't fall asleep and then I collapsed on the trail tomorrow? What if, what if, what if.

"It's time for bed!" Ms. Lewis announced. "I hope that you all have enjoyed this trip so far.

We have many adventures tomorrow, so get some good sleep. Now, I will give a brief description of tomorrow..."

I zoned out for the rest of her speech, my head moving to my stomach. Just thinking about it made me want to throw up. When I realized that everybody was standing up, talking with friends, laughing, and getting into their tents, I turned to Jo. She was already smiling, clearly ready for a night in the woods.

"Come on, Everleigh!" she shouted, heading for our tent.

I reluctantly followed. Once I stood, my legs started to wobble. I steadied myself and shakily followed Jo. I ran through my bedtime routine without brushing my teeth. I didn't want to cause myself to throw up.

I slipped into my sleeping bag and hugged my teddy bear, Bella, close to my heart. I imagined that Bella was my mom, hugging her tight. The thought made the tears that I had been holding back all day slide down my cheeks. I tried to keep it quiet, but obviously Jo heard.

"Are you okay?" she asked. "You seem sad."

"Yeah, I just miss my parents," I sniffled. I hiccuped. Bile rose in my throat and I gagged. I shoved myself out of my sleeping bag. I unzipped the door of the tent and rushed out. It was chilly, but I barely noticed. I ran to the nearest tree and threw up at it's base. It kept coming, and I couldn't stop it. I heard hurried footsteps behind me. I felt a gentle but firm hand on my shoulder. It pulled me back and I finally stopped throwing up. I wiped my mouth on my sleeve. I was sitting up and leaning against a tree, different from the one I had thrown up on. I was staring into Ms. Lewis' face. A very upset Jo lingered behind her.

"What happened?" Ms. Lewis asked.

"I don't know!" I sobbed. Once the tears came, I couldn't stop them.

"Was it something you ate?" Ms. Lewis was very calm, and for some reason, that made me angry.

"No! I didn't even eat anything today!" I sobbed even harder when I came to that realization.

"Do you want to eat something now? I can go get something," Ms. Lewis offered. I nodded, the crying not stopping.

"Can you stay with her? I'm going to get her some bread to soak up some of the extra stomach acid," Ms. Lewis told Jo. Jo just nodded.

"Are you ready to talk?" Jo asked. I shook my head, still crying. So we sat in silence until Ms. Lewis came back with the bread.

I nibbled on it while Ms. Lewis rubbed my back. Jo sat next to me and held my hand.

When all the crying and tears were out, I could tell that Ms. Lewis and Jo really, really wanted to talk. So I did. I told them that I had been nervous. I told them that I didn't eat because of that. I told them everything. Missing my parents, the pandemic, and everything that had been worrying me.

After I was finished, all was quiet until Ms. Lewis broke the tension.

"That is all very normal, Everleigh," she said. "That's happened to me before."

"Me too," Jo added. "Everyone gets nervous at some point in their life."

"You two should go to bed. It's been a long night," Ms. Lewis said.

We obeyed and went back to our tent. I almost laughed out loud! It actually had felt good to throw up, knowing that I had faced my biggest fear, and I was still alive. I had to face my greatest fear, but I conquered it. As I slipped back into my bed, I fell asleep almost immediately.

The next morning, I woke up to gentle shadows of the leaves on the top of the tent. A faint bird sound. It gave me hope. Today was a new day. I was alive, and happy to be on this trip.

I think that me, Jo, and Ms. Lewis all learned something that night. Some things are worth pushing through. Keep going. Never stop fighting for what you need. And most importantly, NEVER give up.

Author's note

I would like to explain a few things about my story. First of all, I would like to explain the background of this story. For the last few months, I have been dealing with anxiety. I was really nervous about going away from my parents, so I decided to have Everleigh live through my experiences. She struggles to keep herself together. She believes that the pandemic is causing this. I mean, who likes the pandemic? I agree with Everleigh when she says that the pandemic ruins everything. It ruined many things for me. Second of all, I would like to explain the origins of Ms. Lewis. In fourth grade, I had the best teacher ever. She encouraged me when I was ready to give up. So thank you so much! Finally, I would like to thank all the people who helped me edit this to make it the best possible. Thank you!

About the Author

Ellie Einfeld is a fifth grader in Grand Rapids. Ever since she read the Harry Potter book series, she has wanted to become a writer. In the fourth grade, she and her friends wrote a 177 page book. They had a lot of encouragement from their teacher, Sra. Silvey. To this day, Ellie still thinks about her teacher's encouraging words to help her write her future books. A special thanks to her mom and dad who helped her edit.

Youth Readers' Choice Winner

Running From the Future
Adi Jain

Bang! The door opened with a screech.

"Johnson, you're up," said the guard, yelling through his megaphone.

The light blinded my eyes as I fell from my bed, waiting to get this all over. The name "Mississippi State Penitentiary" was the sign I had to wake up every day for four months, one week, and four days. My name is Carter Johnson, black, 44 years old and falsely accused of murder. Oh, how I wish this could all be gone, and I could get back to my children and my family.

The memory is so crisp and clear. It was a peaceful and sunny day in good ol' Mississippi, and the sun had slowly started to set. Samantha, my wife, and I were just sitting on our porch, thinking about how good life was and how grateful we were to have each other.

"You know?" My wife said, "I did a lot of bad stuff when I was a kid, but I'm not sure what I did to deserve you."

The kids, the apples of my eye, were playing in the front and having the time of their lives.

"Ring-a-ring-a-rosies, a pocket full of posies, ashes, ashes, we all fall down!"

We lived on a farm just right off Jackson. After mowing lawns and raking leaves for my clients, I had a tiring day and got up to go to the bathroom. I slowly walked to the bathroom and was far away from the porch. I heard some muffled screams coming from the front, but I thought, "It's just the kids." Boy, I didn't know how wrong I was. Kawoosh! We need to get a quieter toilet, I thought. I washed my hands and headed outside.

I couldn't believe what I saw. The shiniest red liquid I have ever seen.

I panicked and quickly ran to get a bat and a phone. Calling 911, I jumped out of the door, landing in a big puddle of blood, splattering all over my pants. My wife is lying on the chair, trying to say my name,

"Cah, Cah, Cath," my wife mumbled. "Cal pewees."

I quickly came to her aid, "HONEY! I'm here. Where are the kids?" My wife was losing blood fast,

"Cah Therr Ther, Carh Ther, loowk," she mumbled, I quickly came back and tended to her,

"Yes, an ambulance is coming. Just hold my hand. Everything will be alright," I said worriedly.

VZOOM!

A gray van zoomed through the rocky road. I could hear yelling from inside it, "DAD, MOM, HELP US!!"

I ran after them, but the van zoomed out of my sight. The police and ambulance soon arrived, put her on a stretcher, but she was pronounced dead on the scene. The police immediately assembled a search party and an AMBER Alert for my three kids, Keisha, 11, Jamal, 7, and Tyra, 6. I sat down on the chair, trying to stop the world from spinning, getting blurry, and my body from trembling. While feeling my heart explode, I tried to remember to breathe at times.

A police officer saw me disoriented and about to collapse.

"We will find your kids. I need you to calm down, ok?" the police officer assured me.

"Arrest him!" a woman shouted from the back.

"I heard them fighting loud all of last night from my house over there!"

I faintly recognized her as the mom of one of our neighbors down the road, but why was she trying to get me arrested?

"Ma'am, please calm down. We are trying to figure out what happened," the officers said.

"His people took the kids, HIS PEOPLE!"

"Ma'am, what do you mean by his people?"

"You know, his people, hurting everyone they see, creating more burdens on officers than there should be."

I was shocked by that racial comment and the lie about our fight.

"Ok, ma'am, we will figure this out. Officer, take her back to her house."

After all the drama, they looked at my track record, and there were two complaints about a domestic disturbance and attempted arson under my name. The evidence was substantial. I had a bat in my hands, matching the wounds on her head, blood splattered on my pants, that crazy woman, and the false claims.

I completely dropped to my knees and started to scream at the top of my lungs, pinching myself, thinking that this was all a nightmare.

"This isn't true! I love my wife, my kids, and my house. I would never do anything to hurt them!"

Police rushed towards me.

"HEY, I have rights! You need a warrant to arrest me!"

The police yelled, "Carter Johnson, you are under arrest for the suspicion of murder, kidnapping, and assault!"

They dragged me off the porch with my hands behind my back, pushing me off the stairs and reading my rights. They shoved me in the car, drove me down to the station. Next was photographs and fingerprints. After two hours, waiting in handcuffs, a guard came out and took me to a cell for several hours. Finally, officials escorted me for the 3-hour drive to the Mississippi State Penitentiary.

I received a hearty welcome by a whole new round of photographs and fingerprints. The guard mumbled, "Looks like you got yourself in a mess."

"I'm innocent!" as I broke down and fell to the floor.

The following day, sitting in the visitor center, I see a court-appointed, 64-year-old lawyer waving at me, who lost almost every murder case. I also found out my trial has been scheduled for September 23, 2019.

"Hey Carter, nice to meet you, my name's Ethan Smith, and I'm your lawyer. Now. TELL. ME. EVERYTHING."

I told him everything that happened from when my wife and I talked till when I got arrested.

He sunk in the chair and thought for a while,

"Ok, we need to gather evidence. Let's see. Did you or your wife have any enemies?"

"No, but her ex-boyfriend from high school had attacked us before, trying to kidnap our youngest child, Tyra, from the playground. He also asked for $5,000 with no police involved."

"Mm-hm, ok, do you know the name of the guy?"

"Walter Allen Schaffer"

"Wait, what?"

"Yes? Is there a problem with that?" I asked suspiciously.

"Yes, it was one of the most difficult cases I've witnessed during my judicial clerkship.

In Walter's youth, he assaulted two people and was involved in many Asian and Black hate crimes. As I recall, he served five years in Louisiana State Prison and got out on parole," Ethan slowly trailed off."

I came back to my cell.

A couple of hours later, while eating lunch, my head was everywhere, thinking about my conversation with Ethan, Samantha, and the kids, making me feel like my entire body was crumbling into dust.

Then, I met Bryce Winston Davis, a psychotic and unstable 39-year-old man serving a life sentence for robberies, black hate crimes, and murder.

"Hey, broskie. Heard about your wife, I'm sorry... for the police who had to see her ugly face!"

That was it. I grabbed Bryce by his collar and smacked the plate across his head.

He dropped to the ground, holding his head and going into the fetal position. Two guards picked him up and radioed guards to take me to my cell.

"This isn't over, broskie! I won't let you leave here alive; forget about your kids." I stood shaken to my core.

"How do you know about my children?" I suspiciously asked. "Let's just say they're not doing the best. Bye broskie, Peace!"

"HEY!" I roared.

Oliver Weinsly, the guard on duty, handcuffed me, taking me back to my cell.

"Stay there. You're not getting out soon. Disrespectful enough, you wife murderer?"

"What's that supposed to mean?"

He kicked my stomach hard.

"The white people made the country that you're ruining by that disgraceful color of skin! Be normal! No food, no water, no daylight, until you respect the people who worked their heads off to make this peaceful country!"

He had kicked me at least four times by now. I slowly realized that they didn't care if I murdered Samantha or not. They were doing this because Samantha was white and I was black! I needed to get out of here.

After two days, full of misery and torture, the blinding prison light shot itself straight into my eyes. I hissed as the room spun. The guard saw me and asked, "Hey, doing ok? Need help?"

That's when I saw Mazzi Valtor Lott, a black 31-year-old guard, the kindest guard in prison.

"Yes, pleas-"

"NO!" shouted Oliver.

"These people are just acting, to get sympathy and care and dodging real prison consequences that they deserve."

"Yes, sir," said Mazzi, lowering his head, and he walked away.

I noticed the "Warden" tag on Oliver's shirt. I observed everyone was avoiding Oliver because he was the cruelest and harassing guard in prison. A couple of minutes later, Mazzi took me to see Ethan.

"Hey, Carter, how's it going?" said Ethan.

"Good, I guess. My life is falling apart, so I'd say I'm doing fine."

"Ok, I have good news for you," Crrrreak!

"Daddy!" The three kids screamed at once.

"Tyra, Jamal, Keisha!!" I yelled in joy.

"We found them on the side of the local Walmart, asking people for a ride," Ethan said. Oh, thank god, I thought, hugging them as hard as I could.

"Are you ok? Did they hurt you?" I worriedly questioned.

Tyra pulled up her right leg's pants, showing a big bandage on her knee. "Please don't worry, I took her to urgent care."

"Thank you, Ethan. I owe you one."

"Dad, the kidnapper, didn't want to hurt us, but when he accidentally hurt Tyra, he panicked and dropped us in the middle of nowhere," traumatized Keisha said.

I hugged the kids again and calmed them down.

"Ok, kids, can you please sit on the couch while Daddy talks to Ethan?"

"Yes, Daddy," all three replied immediately.

"We have 30 days left till the trial, and we haven't had any breakthroughs. We did get a call from McKenna Barker, informing us that she saw that gray van."

"McKenna, McKe- oh! She lives five houses down! Her kids and Keisha often play outside. I've always noticed strange behavior with those kids, and in many instances, covered with bruises. Upon asking, they have replied that they play a lot of sports. Yet, I never found them interested in outdoor activities."

"She said she saw the car model and saw it going by. Also! Walter is ruled out. He has an alibi for being in New York at the time of the murder."

"Finally, some good news," I sighed.

"One more thing that puts me in suspicion, McKenna sounded like someone was forcing her to say this. She was breathing heavily while stuttering in between her words."

"Did she hint anything to you?" I asked.

"She said, if you can't find anything, remember that curtains never cover everything, then hung up the phone abruptly."

Was she being held hostage by the killer and knows who it is? Is she the killer and trying to divert attention?

"Maybe try going to her house and ask her a few questions?" I suggested. "Roger that, matey." Ethan laughed.

The door creaked open.

"You're done. Get up," said Oliver. I stood up and walked to my cell.

The next day came and went, then a week and then another month, and there was no news about McKenna. Morning rollcall and working part-time in the laundry was an everyday routine. I had made some friends behind bars. Before going to bed, I realized each passing day was another day of guilt and harassment. One relief was the kids went to Social Services, where somebody took care of their needs until my trial.

Finally, one day before my trial, Ethan came. He sat down with a sigh of relief.

"Ok, um. I went to McKenna's house. She wasn't there, so the kids opened the door.

Observing everything, I didn't see anything solid, an-" "OK, AND?"

"I then remembered that she said something about curtains, and there were curtains on every window I could see. I searched around and behind every curtain, and I saw a handheld camera on the windowsill. I played it several times back and forth searching to find some evidence, and then one of the recordings told the story about everything that happened that day."

Ethan played the recording.

"Hello, whoever this is. I am here to share the incident of that day when poor Carter Johnson got blamed. My husband, Walter Allen Schaffer, and his friend, Oliver Weinsly, a warden at a prison, are full of hatred towards black people. They hated Carter even more because he is black and married to a white person. One evening in our living room, after a few drinks, I heard them plotting to kill Samantha and kidnap Tyra, Jamal, and Keisha, then frame Carter. My mother-in-law gave her full support to them. She told the officers that you did it all. I called because I needed to save his kids and mine as well. I also need you to give my kids to the police to help them have a better life. Last year, Walter had just come from jail and divorced, and we quickly fell in love. I didn't know he was that bad of a person towards people of color. I might not be here to meet you and help you, but this is my alibi and evidence, and in any way, this may help you, use it."

Wow. I leaned back, and my face beamed. I'm getting out of here! My trial is tomorrow, and I'm going to win.

"Carter, this is good. We can win the trial and get you out of here."

"This is... good. I'll be right back."

I ran to the lunchroom. Mazzi was standing and drinking coffee. "Hey, Mazzi. I'm getting out tomorrow!"

"Really! That's great!"

"Yes, it is. Thanks for helping me."

"No problem, it's my job."

"It was amazing how you stood your ground when they criticized you."

"Doesn't matter. If I am true to myself and live my life, nothing will affect me," said Mazzi, blushing from the compliment.

It was nice to see a kind person who lives his life as he is destined to.

"My wife used to say, sticks and stones may break my bones, but words will never hurt me."

"She must have been a charming lady."

"She was, Mazzi. She was," I sighed.

I went back to my cell, laid back, and slept graciously.

The following day, I got up, looked at the reflection of the toilet water to see myself, and smiled, the biggest smile a person could smile. I got ready in my suit, and Mazzi opened the cell gate to take me to Ethan.

"Are you ready, Carter," asked Mazzi.

"Readier than a lion waiting to pounce. ROAR!" I shouted. Mazzi laughed and wished me good luck

Ethan was standing at the entrance of the door, sticking his hand out to shake my hand. "Let's go! The trial is at 10 o'clock. It's already nine-thirty," Ethan worriedly rushed. "Ok, ok. Ethan. First, I need to thank you. You have been the greatest help. You were by me during the tough times. You supported my kids. You stood me up when I fell. That's what a friend does, not a lawyer, a friend."

"Thank you, Carter. You have been a very nice friend to me and were patient throughout the whole process and were calm at the bad news, and ecstatic at the good news. I will support you in your whole journey and after that as well. Now, we are running late. Let's talk more in the car on the way to the courthouse. Also, I have a small surprise for you."

"Phwwwwwhht," Ethan whistled.

The kids came running from behind the door.

"DADDY! You're here! We all missed you so much!" they all yelled as they jumped in my arms.

"HEY, GUYS! How have you been?

"Good!" they all said at once.

"Tyra, how is your leg?" I questioned.

"Better! Now I can do cartwheels again. Wanna see?" she cutely asked. "I would love to!"

"WOO-HOO! GO TYRA! GO TYRA!" we all shouted at once.

"I'm sorry I haven't been there for you as much as I should have. Tell you what, after I get out today, we can go get ICE CREAM!"

"Yay, Dad!" shouted Jamal and Tyra.

"Guys." Keisha spoke, "We should let Dad rest today. We can start all the fun tomorrow."

"Thank you, Keisha. Tomorrow is going to be FUN-DAY!"

"YAY! We are so glad you are back, Dad."

"Guys, we got to go now, kids. Social Services will take care of you for a couple of hours, till we are back. Stay strong, kiddos," Ethan told them.

"Good Luck, Dad."

I left the prison feeling proud, energetic, and grateful. I sat in the car and buckled up.

"This is what you have been waiting for, Carter."

"Yes, I have."

"Let's go, driver." Ethan hurried.

We left the prison, and I rested my head on the headrest and thought, I have my kids and friends and family supporting me. We will win this case and show others that people of color have every right to have freedom, liberty, and justice.

As Thomas Jefferson, a white man, wrote in the Declaration of Independence, "We hold these truths to be self-evident, that all men are created equal, that they are endowed by their Creator with certain unalienable Rights, that among these are Life, Liberty and the Pursuit of Happiness."

I gleamed as I looked out the window, thinking about when four months ago I was in a cop car, an arrested man. I'm coming back as a free man who can finally be himself.

About the Author

Adi Jain, a sixth grader, is a passionate reader and a fictional story writer. He has the most creative ideas for writing. He has written and composed small stories and poems, which have won many awards. His recent story imagination is *Running From The Future*. This story was inspired by the tragic and violent events that are happening around us based on race. He feels these incidents destroy our energy, our inner peace, and our values. Adi chose to express that in a form of a story to make people understand that these havocking and controversial events increase hatred and decrease humanity. He feels that we are all collectively liberators of equality, and we all have indistinguishable existence and rights. #BlackLivesMatter.

Youth Published Finalist

Where I Belong
Amelia Bogertman

"And now we eat!" Nonno Alben finally sits down with us at the dinner table, after a while of cooking. He's my grandfather. This is the biggest feast of the year. "Buon appetito!" Every year my family has a big Italian feast to celebrate an incredible life. "*Cibo, cibo, così buono! Fatto da Nonno Alben,*" says Nonna Sofia. She is the oldest, the wisest. Mamma says I have her intelligence, optimism, and her curly brown hair. I love her oh so much, and I hope that I'll never lose her, for she is the light that shines on my path.

My name is Giulia Romano. I live in Portorosso, with my mamma, papa, and my big brother, Marco. My *famiglia*(family) all live here, too. "*Grazie,* to everyone who is a Romano," says my 19 year old *cugina*(cousin), Greta. We all bow our heads and pray. I've always been a shy girl, but when I'm with my family, I feel like myself. I'm about to start a new school in Villetta, a town not too far from here. My house back in Viterbo burned down in a fire, so now we live at Nonno and Nonna's here in Portorosso. *I'm nervous to start my new school. I won't know anyone*! Since my *famiglia* is poor, this school was a big purchase. All the other kids are probably super rich.

After we prayed, everyone dug into the delicious food; turkey, brussel sprouts, mushrooms, pasta rigatoni, strawberries, and Mamma's famous key lime pie.

After the feast, we stampede into the living room, and lounge around the sofas, talking, and relaxing. After talking with the adults, I go and play with my cugina Rosee, and cugina Amara. They are the twin babies of the family. I just love them, and they love me, too. After a while, the older relatives, including me, gather up to play hide-and-go-seek. Greta counts first. 1, 2, 3, 4, all the way to 50. Like little mice, my cugino Leonardo and I team up together and creep into the washroom. My tiny body manages to fit in the washer, and Leonardo hides amongst towels in the towel closet, fighting for space. We can hear all the kids that Greta finds. Lorenzo and Alessandro, Kayla and Aurora, Alice and Gabriele, and then lastly, Leonardo and me.

"I've gotcha, Giulia!" Greta opens up the washer roughly, and Lorenzo finds Leonardo in the closet.

"You guys win! Buon lavoro! Good job, good job," Kayla congratulates us.

We play famiglia games all night. After all the relatives go home, my famiglia stays at Nonno and Nonna's house for the night.

"Buona notte, mia dolce Giulia," Nonna Sofia says, her voice trembling sleepily.

"Buona notte to you too, Nonna," I kiss her on the cheek, and Nonno Alben comes in and tucks me into the guest bed. Then after a hug, he winks at me and pushes Nonna Sofia out in her wheelchair. As I lie there in the dark, I think about my incredible life. I think of sweet Nonno and Nonna. I think of the *deliziosa cena* that we ate that night. But then I think about Nonna's hands trembling, and her in a wheelchair. It occurs to me that Nonna is really old. 97! I wonder if she will live any longer. I try to shove the thought out of my head like an unwelcome guest. I drift to sleep, peacefully, my brain overflowing like the fountain at the plaza in the center of Porto Rosso. I really hope Nonna Sofia is okay.

About a month later, I start school in Villeta. All the students are perfect. They all have wavy hair, but mine is scraggly. They have perfect uniforms, but mine is stained. They all seem popular, and I'm dull. The cool kids walk around like toucans; vibrant, drawing attention to themselves, getting everyone to look and be amazed. I'm a squirrel; your everyday animal. Not drawing attention, dull, not very interesting. The toucans stare at me, unimpressed. I try to brush off the dust and be myself. *You can do this, Giulia. You can be confident. You've got this. Now go and make friends with a toucan.*

Epic fail! *I didn't talk to a single kid! I'm shy, and weird! I can't stand this.* At this moment I want to move! But this is where I belong! I can't leave Portorosso. As I walk home from school, I cry. There are lots of things to cry about. My *famiglia* is poor, they can't even pay for me to ride a bus, nor buying me a fresh new uniform. I don't fit in. And worse, when I get home, Nonna Sofia is lying on the couch in our house, looking very sick.

She can't die! Not now! She is the only one who understands me. "Mamma, Papa, what happened-" I stammered.

"She had a stroke," Said Papa. My mouth falls open. "Wha, how, when, no!" I fall to my knees, sobbing. Mamma hugs me close. "Is she alive?"

"Giulia, my little Giulia," Mamma closes her eyes, folds her hands, and turns toward Nonna Sofia.

"What is going on?" I whine.

"My wife is dead. Mamma was trying to tell you. She had a stroke after you left for Villeta, and we went to the hospital and Doctor Vincent said that she is dead, or at least very, very sick. We couldn't afford paying for a hospital room for the night. I'm so sorry, my Giulia, but we have to let her go." I cry harder, dead inside, like Nonna Sofia.

"Can I be alone with her for a second?" I ask. Nonno Alben nods. My famiglia leaves the room, and as I sit down next to her, she opens her eyes, but there is still no hope. She might have been awake now, but we all knew that even if she was living now, she would pass on quickly after.

"Giulia. Is it you?" Nonna Sofia whispers.

"Nonna, I-"

"Hush, my little girl. I know what happened at school. Mamma told me that she couldn't afford new things for my Giu Giu. Why, Giulia?"

"Nonna Sofia, we all know we're poor. We can't afford things. The money is slipping from our hands quicker than sound travels from our mouths to someone's ears. Who knows what's coming next. The house? Food? The *macchina*? We can't lose the car! Oh, Nonna. Why do you have to leave at a time like this?" I was desperate for comfort and help.

"Oh, Giulia. Don't worry. I'm leaving peace and love where I used to be. Take my blessing, and I promise things will change. Stay calm, and know your Nonna loves you. Goodbye, Giulia." Like a whale swimming into the deep and disappearing, Nonna Sofia lets the darkness take her and she leaves us. I sobbed, trying to let the fact that people die wash over me. Mamma, Marco, Papa, and Nonno Alben all comforted me. We had a group *abbraccio*, but it was no group hug without Nonna.

After a sad week, we managed to push through. School didn't get better. We needed to carpool with friends, but I had none. One day, the best one of all, I met a boy named Eduardo.

"Hi, I'm Eduardo Bianchi. And you are?" He asked.

"I'm Giulia, Giulia Romano."

"Oh! A Romano. I saw the newspaper. So sorry about your Nonna," Eduardo pleaded. "I let it go, Eduardo. I'm just," I pause, wrinkling my eyebrows at the floor.

"Fine."

He purses his lips, and Mr. Colombo drones on and on about World War II. Me and Eduardo groan and roll our eyes. We smile, and laugh and whisper to each other for the rest of the class. At lunch, I sit alone, of course.

"Hey! You are Julian, right? Or was it Juliette?" Eduardo plops down next to me. After an hour of chatting and he couldn't remember my name?

"Yeah, how'd you not remember?" I look at him, confused.

"Oh, I have communication issues," He grins.

"And how does that connect to memory loss?" I am so confused now.

"I've got that, too. I'm a special needs kid. Go ahead, be annoyed and make fun of it." He looks down at his lower body, as I just notice his wheelchair. How did I not see it?

"Well Eduardo, I don't care. You're perfect the way you are. Don't let others discourage you. Do what you want. Kids in wheelchairs and kids with special needs and kids with both can do anything. They can play basketball, football, you name it. You can do it! Believe in yourself. If others don't like it, that's their loss. You can do anything!"

I stand on top of the table, protesting. After that, he just stares at me, along with everyone else. Some people laugh, but Eduardo just stares up at me, mesmerized, mouth wide open, and nodding. I sit back down, realizing that I went too far. We exchange looks, and laugh again. My life gets better. My Nonna's spirit and gifts that she left for us when she passed away would always stay with me. Eduardo and I were best friends. And guess what? He was new, too! My Nonna flew away, letting go, and that made me see that I could grow wings, too, and fly far away and meet her in the middle. All I had to do was be me, and help others. Things can get better, just give it time. I scooped up Nonna's gratitude and will hold it close for as long as I will live. I am lucky, even if I don't seem that way. I'm lucky because I have people by my side, staying with me through the thick of it. I'm glad that I'm where I belong.

The End.

About the Author

Amelia Bogertman is almost 11 years old, and is always typing stories. She was born in West Michigan, has lived in Colorado and now lives in the Grand Rapids area. She enjoys listening to music, dancing, skiing, reading, running, singing, and playing with her neighbors. She and her neighbors do a lot of activities and businesses around the neighborhood such as baking, pet sitting, and sledding. She is the middle child, and has an older sister and younger brother. Amelia is very excited to have made it to the top ten!

Youth Published Finalist

Journey to the Elder Cat
Colette Horvath

There was a burst of light and a bang. After I woke up, my mother was gone...

I was born in a broken-down tool shed with my five other siblings. I wish I could say that the tool shed was a good home for a cat, but it wasn't. There were holes in the roof so when the sky cried we all got wet, and when the drops hit my fur they felt like little knives. Every night, because I was the eldest, my mother and I went out to hunt. We would find rats, mice, and squirrels to bring home to our family. We had just caught a rat when there was a burst of light and a huge bang. I felt a sudden pain in my side and everything went black.

When I woke up it was dark and my mother was gone. I knew I had to get back to my siblings. So I sniffed around to find the rat we had killed. I found it and bolted for home.

"Where are they?" Finn asked. He was the youngest of us.

"I don't know," replied Marie, the second eldest. She was trying to sound strong through her fear.

"I am sure Kane and mother are fine," said Rayla, the middle cat, in an uncertain tone. "They probably just chased an animal a long way from home."

Kane and their mother had been gone all night and all morning.

The sun was starting to rise. I was so grateful for the sun. But my stomach was empty. I knew I needed to eat but thinking about eating the rat - the last thing my mother touched - was almost too much to bear. So I did what my mother taught me to do. I found a pile of leaves to hide in and waited and waited and waited, but no animal came. At that point I was desperate so I found a berry bush. The berries were very sour but they helped with the pain in my stomach. As I continued on, my fear grew and grew that my siblings would not be okay when I got to the tool shed. Little did I know that when I got there one of my siblings would not be okay.

The second youngest, Leah, had been quiet all night and all morning. She had been feeling very tired and dizzy but she didn't want to add to the stress everybody was already feeling.

"Leah, are you okay?" Marie asked.

"I don't know," she replied.

Marie went over to look at Leah.

"Oh no!" Marie said after looking Leah over. "You have ancirea!" If you didn't know, ancirea is a deadly disease that wild cats get. The only cure is if three of the sick cat's relatives go to the Elder Cat and exchange one dead rat for the antidote.

"But there are only three of us here, not including Leah," said Rayla. "Who will stay with her?" They would just have to wait until Kane and their mother got home. If they ever did...

I started to recognize the places around our tool shed. The steep grassy hill that my siblings and I would play on. The ancient boulder I would hide behind at bedtime. I knew I was close. When I saw the tool shed, I couldn't have been happier. But immediately when I walked in I knew something was wrong. Everyone was quiet.

"Hello!" I yelled after plopping down the rat.

"Kane!" everyone shouted as they scampered up to me.

"But where's Leah?" I asked.

"She's sleeping... she has ancirea," Marie said uneasily.

"Oh no, we must leave immediately! Finn, Marie, and I will go. Rayla, you stay with Leah. I already have this rat. Are you ready?" I asked my siblings.

"Yes!" they mewed.

"Wait," Rayla said. "Where is mother?"

"I don't know, there was a burst of light and a huge bang and I felt a sudden pain in my side, and the next thing I knew she was gone."

Everyone was silent.

"I don't know where she is right now, but right now she'd want us to get going," I said. We started on our journey to the Elder Cat.

"Are we there yet?" Finn pestered.

"For the ninth time, no, we are not there yet and won't be for a while," I answered reluctantly. Finn pouted for a while but got over it quickly.

"Do you still remember the directions Rayla told us?" Marie asked.

"Yep: over the rolling hills, through the bat cave, an island in the middle of Lake Craning is where the Elder Cat lies down," I replied.

"Look over there!" Marie exclaimed. "Rolling hills!"

Finn scampered away as Marie and I took in the view. The sun was setting and we wished the picture in the sky could stay the way it was forever.

"This might be the last time we see the sun before we go into the bat cave," I said to Marie.

"Ugh, I don't want to go into a cave," she said resentfully.

"Speaking of the bat cave, there it is..." I said.

Sure enough on the next hill, there was a dark hole embedded in its grass. Finn rejoined us and we ventured into the cave.

The first thing that we noticed were the torches on the walls because each one flared into life as we approached. We didn't know why it was called the bat cave, but we would find out soon. We kept on walking until we made it to a huge pitch-black room.

"What's that?" asked Finn.

"What's what?" Marie and I replied.

"That squeaking noise..." he replied. "I don-"

"WHY HAVE YOU COME HERE?", a strange voice interrupted me.

The voice echoed in the darkness. Marie stepped forward timidly and said, "We need to get to the Elder Cat... our sister is sick."

"I should have known," growled the voice. Suddenly, more torches burst into flame, and in front of us sat a huge bat on a throne of bone.

"I will show you the way out if you solve my riddle, but if you guess wrong your spine will be added to my throne. Are you ready?" the bat snarled.

I started to answer but he interrupted me again.

"Ha-ha, I don't care! Now the riddle is: *What is always coming but never here?* I am giving you one minute, oh and oops I already started it!"

I turned to Marie.

"I know I've heard this one before," she said.

"Let's see if I can jog your memory. Umm... okay, pineapple... Santa... door... cave... tomorrow..." I offered.

"Oh, that's it! It's tomorrow!"

"Tomorrow!" we shouted.

"Ugghh..." the bat groaned in complaint. "Now I have to let you go," he said, sulking. We didn't want to celebrate until we got out of the cave alive. Suddenly bats flew down from the ceiling and opened a hidden stone door. The three of us escaped the bat cave.

When we came out there was a grassy plain as far as the eye could see. But in the distance, we could just make out a lake with an island in the middle of it. We leaped with joy! We were one step closer to the Elder Cat.

We walked up to the lake and found it was a lot bigger than we anticipated. There was a small sailboat, but none of us knew how to sail. We got on anyway and set out for the island. It started out rough; the water kept splashing onto the boat and freaking us out. Soon we got used to it and quickly made our way toward the island. Once we arrived we really didn't know what to do. All that was on the island was a small hill. And of course, Finn had to climb it. And as soon as he set paw on it, the hill began to... uncurl?... revealing the Elder Cat!

"I offer two answers to anything, and one object of your choice," the Elder Cat said in a sleepy voice.

"I know exactly what I am going to ask," I told Marie. I faced the Elder Cat. "What happened to my mother?"

"Ahh, yes. She was captured by some humans, for other humans to buy her for a pet."

"Oh," I whispered. "But what were those lights, and the bang?"

"Well the light was coming from a car and the bang was a tranquilizer gun."

"Oh... for the object, we need the antidote for ancirea and I have the rat right here." I nosed the rat and the Elder Cat gave me the antidote in exchange.

"Now, would you like a ride home?" the Elder Cat asked.

"Yes please," Marie said. The Elder Cat stretched out and told us to get on his back. We did and we flew all the way home.

Once we all got off the Elder Cat in front of our tool shed I turned around to thank him, but he was gone. As we walked in we found Rayla pacing back and forth across the floor while Leah was sleeping.

"We got the antidote!" I cheered and put it down in front of me.

We quickly gave Leah the antidote. I watched her face as sunlight crept across the floor toward us. Just as it reached her, she opened her eyes and I knew everything would be okay.

About the Author

Colette Horvath is a 5th grader in Byron Center, Michigan. She has six pets and four human family members. Colette loves to read, write, draw, and play with her brother. She aspires to be a professional author someday. Her favorite foods are bacon and tacos (though not together).

Youth Published Finalist

Ciara and the Ring of Fires
Sevie Roddy

Ciara closed her reading assignment with a thump. Her friend Emme must get much more fascinating homework at St. Peter's School of Magic. Emilia Jones was Ciara's best friend, but they saw each other less after Emme's parents sent her to St. Peter's School of Magic. Ciara sighed, knowing she mustn't let her jealousy get the better of her. She scribbled in the last bubble in her workbook, feeling better about the assignment now that she had finished it.

Suddenly, Ciara heard a clang.

"Good grief, Nicko!" She huffed under her breath. Her brother must have broken something.

She raced to the kitchen, her woolen socks slipping and sliding on the tiles like skates on ice.

"Help!" Nicko shouted.

At last, Ciara reached Nicko. He was wildly swinging a frying pan at a large black blob floating just above the counter.

What in the world?! Ciara thought. Nothing, not even her exotic science class, had prepared her for this. She wondered if the blob was dangerous. She couldn't let it hurt Nicko! She grabbed another frying pan and swung it at the blob. To her horror, the blob seemed to melt around the frying pan, sucking it into its vast darkness and tugging at Ciara's arm.

Ciara pulled at the frying pan, to no avail. Her little brother watched her, not sure what to do. Ciara yanked harder. The blob seemed to be growing around her hand, sucking her in little by little. Soon she was floating, legs in the air.

At the last moment, when Ciara was sure the blob would suck her in completely, Nicko leaped up and grabbed her feet.

Nicko held on tightly, but the blob seemed to be pushing him out. Nicko let go of Ciara's feet with a groan, and she disappeared into the darkness.

"No!" He shouted. "Ciara, come back!"

Ciara tore at the gooey blackness around her, but the blob would not let her out.

Suddenly, there was a blinding flash of light. The blob disappeared, seeming to dissolve into thin air. Ciara fell to the ground.

"Ouch!" She muttered.

She scrambled to her feet and dusted herself off. Then she looked up and gasped. Three figures in black cloaks stood in front of her, muttering to themselves.

"Is she the one?" The thin one asked.

"She doesn't seem as bright as we thought," said the small one. "She knows nothing of the simple blob illusion."

"Well, excuse me!" Ciara snapped. "I never took magic lessons! My parents forbade us."

"She speaks!"

"To us!"

"Is she not scared?"

"No, I am not scared!"

Ciara spluttered indignantly.

"Hmph," said the figure in front of Ciara. "She is an ignorant child. She speaks without respect."

"Why should I respect you?" Ciara asked. "I don't even know you!"

"Ha! The child knows not who we are!"

"Or where we stand!"

"She does not know anything!" Ciara was getting annoyed.

"Why did you bring me here if you're not even going to speak directly to me?" She asked.

"Us?" asked the one in front of her. "Oh, we did not bring you here. The blob illusion did."

Ciara decided not to speak anymore. Perhaps she would understand more if she had gone to St. Peter's School of Magic as Emme did.

"I am Alexandrius Drake," said the tall figure in front of Ciara. "Follow me."

Not knowing what else to do, Ciara trailed after him. The other figures stayed back, still gossiping about Ciara. Alexandrius led Ciara down a dark corridor that resembled an enlarged wormhole. She made sure to remember where they turned or entered a side passage so that she might have a chance at escape.

At last, they reached their destination. An ominous door loomed over Ciara and Alexandrius like a cat over its prey. But Alexandrius was not deterred. He pressed his hand to the side of the door, and it swung open smoothly. Ciara followed him into a beautifully furnished chamber, covered from floor to ceiling with intricate patterns etched in the finest gold.

Alexandrius beckoned her over to a lovely golden chair adorned with velvet cushions. "Sit," he commanded.

Ciara sat down in the chair. Alexandrius snapped his fingers. Around his neck, an amber and gold pendant began to glow with a soft, eerie light. The ornate gold and amber chandelier that lit the room slowly dimmed. Soon the only remaining light came from Alexandrius's pendant. The pendant's light was somehow calming, almost hypnotizing, and Ciara felt herself falling into a trance.

Suddenly, Ciara remembered Nicko. All alone in the Smiths' mansion, Nicko must be searching for her, telling himself that she would return home any minute now. Soon their parents would be home. Ciara had to get back home. Fast.

Ciara decided to pretend to become hypnotized. She did not want anyone to control her mind. Emme had told her about the Magicians of Fire, a notorious group of magic makers who used evil illusions to control the minds of others. Alexandrius could be one of them.

Ciara felt something pressing against her brain, trying to enter. It was a strange feeling because she knew it was just an illusion. Ciara shoved back against it. Even so, she felt it slowly seeping into her mind like water through a cloth. What should I do? She thought frantically.

Suddenly she realized that her mental barrier grew stronger the more she thought about other things.

She thought of Nicko and how he always managed to get himself into trouble in the simplest of situations. Sure enough, the more she thought of Nicko, the stronger her mental barrier became.

Finally, after what seemed like hours but was likely only a few minutes, the invader left.

The pendant dimmed, and the chandelier returned. Ciara opened her eyes.

"Come with me," Alexandrius commanded.

Ciara realized that there should be something different about her or Alexandrius would realize that he had not hypnotized her. She decided that it would be best to pretend that she was his apprentice.

"Yes, Master," Ciara said.

To her surprise, Alexandrius nodded approvingly. Together, they returned to the corridor where Alexandrius's two accomplices were waiting for them.

"How did it go?" Asked the thin one.

"Very well," Alexandrius answered. "The girl is my apprentice now." He turned to Ciara. "Apprentice, what is your name?"

"My name is Ciara, good Master," Ciara answered.

"Well, Ciara, welcome to the mansion of the Magicians of Fire!" The thin figure exclaimed. "I am Narsucius Blank."

"And I am Lificius Dark," said the smallest one. "The others are out at the moment; you will meet them later."

"Now it is time for the final ritual," Alexandrius said mysteriously. "Follow me, Ciara."

"Yes, master," Ciara responded.

She accompanied Alexandrius farther down the corridor, past the door to the gold chamber.

Finally, they got to the end of the corridor. Right in front of Ciara and Alexandrius were the most beautiful double doors Ciara had ever seen. They were translucent gold with a mixture of red, green, blue, light pink, and dark gray. The colors swirled together like waves in the sea.

"These are the doors of The Everything," Alexandrius explained to his mesmerized apprentice. "The Guardians can read the door, and it will tell everything they wish to know."

"Master, who are the Guardians?" Ciara asked tentatively.

"The Guardians are the seven Magical people who control the seven elements." "Oh?"

"The Guardians are the Witch of Life, the Alchemist of Stone, the Wizard of Water, the Fairy of the Air, Talestina, Elezmere, and I."

"Who is Elezmere?"

"He is the leader of the Keepers of the Nothing."

"Who is Talestina?"

"She is the leader of the Guardians."

"Wow. . ."

Alexandrius sighed.

"Ciara, you are my apprentice. In seven years, you will be a Magician of Fire."

"Yes, Master."

Ciara nodded sadly. She wished she could be an apprentice to someone else. Talestina or Elezmere sounded cool. But most of all, Ciara wanted the Witch of Life. Her friend Emme had told her a bit about Witchery. She said that Ciara would make a good witch. But Emme had talked the most about the Alchemist of Stone. It was clear that she wished to be his apprentice. Emme was already a great Alchemist; she had once turned a simple bead bracelet into gold and revived her dead hamster.

Alexandrius turned to Ciara.

"Are you ready for the ritual?" He asked.

"Y-yes, Master," Ciara responded nervously.

Alexandrius pulled something out of his long cloak. It was a handprint on a pink oval- shaped stone. Alexandrius didn't seem to be in the mood for conversation anymore, so Ciara didn't ask what it was. Alexandrius pressed the handprint to the golden doors. They swung open in a beautiful rainbow of color. Alexandrius advanced through the doors, and Ciara stepped out behind him.

There, in front of them, was a truly magnificent courtyard. It was filled with luscious green grass and surrounded by a tall stone wall. In the center of the courtyard, a large iron ring was half-buried in the ground. It had small pebbly paths winding through it like snakes. Six pedestals, each holding a fire of a different color, were half-buried around the ring, and one pedestal with a rainbow fire stood at its center.

The dancing lights of the fires reflected on the stone wall around the courtyard.

"Wow," Ciara breathed.

"This is the courtyard of all magic," Alexandrius told her. "If you touch one of the fires, you will change forever. You will have a yearning to learn all magic of that sort, and you will learn it with ease."

"Which type of magic does each fire represent?" Ciara asked.

"The green fire is of life and Witchery," Alexandrius began. "The gray fire is of stone and Alchemy. The pink fire is of Fairies and air. The black fire is of the Keepers and the Nothing. The red fire is of Magicians. The blue fire is of Wizardry and water. The rainbow fire is of the Guardians and everything. It is so powerful that it will reject anyone who is not fit to become a Guardian."

"Wow," Ciara gasped. "So much magic."

"Yes," Alexandrius agreed. "Now that you know about the Ring of Fires, you may complete the ritual. Walk carefully toward the red fire of Magicians. Make sure you don't touch any of the other ones."

"Yes, master," Ciara said.

She trembled with excitement and fear. Could she do it? Could she defy her master and touch the green fire of Witchery? Then she remembered Emme's words.

"I know you want to be a witch," Emme had said. "You can become a witch. You can do anything if you set your mind to it."

I can, Ciara thought. *I can become a witch.*

Then she stepped toward the green fire. She seemed to be going toward the red fire, but just as she passed the green fire, she stretched her hand out and touched its brilliant flames.

"No!" Alexandrius screeched. "You have no idea what you just did!"

Oh, I do, Ciara thought. She felt more alive now than ever before. Her curly brown hair was standing straight up. Green sparks shot out of her hands and dress.

Alexandrius raced toward her, his pendant glowing. But as he leaped toward her, his feet seemed to slow.

Ciara's whole life flashed before her eyes. Then she saw her future, a young girl mixing herbs with a strange woman, probably the Witch of Life.

Then she heard a voice in her head.

"Do it!" The voice said.

Ciara didn't know what she was supposed to do. But whoever had spoken to her seemed to be guiding her. She reached out and grabbed a single green flame from the fire.

Ciara scooped the flame into the palm of her hand and hurled it at Alexandrius. He screeched like a cat as it hit him in the face. He fell to the ground and said nothing more.

"He has gone to the Void," the voice in Ciara's head said. "He will not be able to cause any more trouble there. Now, will you come with me? I am the Witch of Life. I am ready to be your master."

Ciara thought for a moment. She'd had enough of this "master" business for one day, but an apprenticeship to the Witch of Life seemed promising.

"Okay," Ciara said nervously. "I'll go."

"Good," said the Witch.

The courtyard swirled around Ciara for a split second. When it stopped, she found herself in a treehouse high in the forest.

"Hello, Ciara," said a voice. Ciara spun around.

The woman that she had seen from her future was standing behind her. "H-hello, master," Ciara stuttered.

"No need for all that formality," the Witch replied kindly. "You can call me Val."

"Okay, Val," Ciara replied. "What would you like me to do?"

"I need you to get ready to become my apprentice," Val told her. "I know your parents. Your mother had a bad experience with magic, and your parents forbade you from using it at all costs."

"Yes," Ciara agreed. "They won't let me become your apprentice."

"I need you to show them something," Val replied.

She stepped into another room for a moment. She returned holding an ornate cup made of carved animal bones and leaves. Inside the cup was a single green flame.

"Wow," Ciara breathed. "You have more of the green fire."

"Yes, I do," Val agreed. "Take this home to your parents, and they will let you be my apprentice."

Ciara nodded. As she took the cup, the room whirled around her, and she was back home.

"Ciara!" Mrs. Smith was delighted to see her daughter.

"Cici!" Nicko was even more delighted.

"Hi, Mom, Nicko!" Ciara exclaimed.

She set the cup down behind her so she could hug them. Once they had finished hugging her, Ciara brought out the cup.

"May I be the Witch of Life's apprentice?" She asked softly.

"Th-this is from the Witch of Life?" Mrs. Smith asked very quietly.

"Yes."

"Oh, Cici," Mrs. Smith sighed. "You know what I think of magic."

Ciara had a sinking feeling in her stomach. Then her dad came into the room. "Ciara. . ." he looked stern.

Ciara prepared for the worst.

"I think that's a great idea!" Mr. Smith exclaimed.

"What?!" Mrs. Smith was appalled. "Seriously?!"

"Very seriously," Mr. Smith told her. "I think this is a great opportunity for young Ciara.

I've known the Witch of Life. She won't expose Ciara to danger until she's ready."

"Rubbish!" Mrs. Smith exclaimed. "All those magic makers are the same! Remember my sister? She was an apprentice to the Fairy of Air, and she never came back!"

The whole family was silent for a moment. Then Nicko spoke up.

"I think the Fairy of Air made a mistake," he said quietly. "She was very young. Too young to control the air all by herself. She needed help, and she thought she could find it in an apprentice."

"She was wrong," Ciara added. "But I think the Witch of Life is different. She has more experience than the Fairy of Air did, so she knows what she's doing."

"True, but how do you know things won't get dangerous?" Mrs. Smith asked.

"I saw the future," Ciara told her mother. "I saw myself mixing herbs with the Witch of Life. Unless you think mixing herbs is dangerous, I should be fine."

"Hmm. . ." Mrs. Smith thought about this for a moment. "How did you see the future?"

"I'll tell you later. But please, please, please, let me be the apprentice to the Witch of Life."

"Alright, dear. But promise to be careful."

"I promise."

Later that night, Ciara curled up in her bed, the green flame from the Witch of Life glowing soothingly on her nightstand. She wondered if she had done the right thing by throwing the fire at Alexandrius Drake. Then she remembered what Emme had told her.

"Sometimes, in magic, you have to eliminate the evil for the good to succeed," Emme had said. "You mustn't let that make you feel sad. Just remember that you are helping the greater good."

As long as Emme was her friend, Ciara knew everything would be all right.

About the Author

Sevie Roddy is ten years old and lives in Ann Arbor, Michigan, with her parents, sister, and pet hamster. She enjoys playing violin and reading books. She likes cats, dogs, and aye-ayes. She wants to be a biologist when she grows up.

Spanish Language Youth Judges' Choice Winner

Carrera de bicicleta

Elijah Kuiper

El viento soplaba contra mi cara y los insectos pasaban volando a mi lado, entrándome en los ojos. Escuché los pájaros en los árboles y el satisfactorio sonido de las ruedas de mi bicicleta rodando por el pavimento. Estaba en una de mis velocidades más rápidas. Agarré el manillar con fuerza. "¡Cuidado con esa zanja de ahí arriba, amigo!" Mi papá gritó detrás de mí. Pero ya la había visto y la esquivé.

Era un típico paseo en bicicleta al mediodía en un día de verano, atravesando el sendero en el bosque, con mi papá corriendo detrás de mí en caso de accidente. La mayoría de mis amigos asumían que sabia montar bien mi bicicleta ya que ahora tengo 7 años, pero nunca me había interesado aprender.

Hace un mes, me enteré de que habría una gran carrera aquí mismo en mi vecindario, en la península superior de Michigan. No quiero pensar en lo que hubieran hecho mis amigos si yo no participaba.

Pero esa no era la verdadera razón por la que estaba ingresando a la carrera. Como la mayoría de las personas que competían, yo buscaba la victoria, el premio peso en monedas metálicas. Además, como la mayoría de la gente, yo también tenía algo en mente y para lo que quería usar el premio. La mayoría de las personas en la Península Superior tienen árboles cerca de su casa o en su propiedad, y yo tengo un roble de mi patio trasero. Ha sido mi sueño durante años desde que nos mudamos aquí, el construir una casa en ese árbol, pero nunca habíamos tenido el dinero. Esta era mi oportunidad.

Empecé a acelerar de solo pensar en ello, mis ojos lejanos en una mirada soñadora. Eso era lo único en lo que estaba pensando

"¡Isaías, ten cuidado!"

Desperté de soñar despierto para ver que estaba acelerando fuera del camino.

¡¡¡CRASH!!!

Mi bicicleta chocó con el árbol más cercano y salí volando del manillar, y me golpeé la cabeza contra el suelo del bosque. Mi papá llegó corriendo al bosque, pero yo estaba demasiado mareado para notar que intentaba ayudarme. Me tambaleé sobre mis pies, mareado. Entonces vi mi bicicleta. La rueda estaba doblada y a punto de caerse, y el manillar estaba torcido.

"Oh, amigo, ¿estás bien?" Preguntó mi papá.

"Creo que sí ..." dije haciendo una mueca. Saboree sangre en mi boca. "Pero mi bicicleta no está bien."

"Podemos arreglarlo, estoy seguro. No te preocupes por eso."

Todavía no le había dicho a mi papá lo que planeaba hacer con el dinero, no quería preocuparlo con el costo. Además, no estoy seguro lo que el pensaría acerca de mis planes, pero probablemente los suyos no incluían una casa en el árbol. "Digamos que hemos practicado suficiente por hoy." Dijo mi papá, y trató de levantar mi bicicleta rota y ayudarme a caminar al mismo tiempo. Debido a esto, varias veces dejó caer la bicicleta en la acera y nos sentamos a pensar cómo llevar la bicicleta al auto.

En ese momento, se nos acercó un hombre vestido con ropa vieja y gastada y sin zapatos. Tenía el pelo curtido y el rostro arrugado, y la clase de ojos tristes que se ven en las personas sin hogar.

"Oye", dijo. "¿Necesitan ayuda con esto?"

"Eso sería bueno", dijo mi papá, mientras yo le daba una sonrisa.

"Por lo que vi, tuviste un gran accidente allí". Él dijo. "¿Entrenando para algo?"

"Sí, para la carrera que viene a la ciudad", dije. "Todavía estoy aprendiendo, como puedes ver.

"Seguro. También para mí fue difícil. Sigue practicando. Ya lo aprenderás." Hablamos el resto del camino de regreso al auto, yo, mi papá y el hombre. Cuando llegamos allí, mi papá me ayudó a sentarme y se subió. Bajó la ventanilla de su vieja camioneta mientras el hombre cargaba mi bicicleta para ponerla en la parte de atrás.

"Muchas gracias", dijo mi papa.

"Sí, sí, no hay problema. Buena suerte en la carrera, grandullón." Me miró desde el asiento trasero con una sonrisa. "Mejórate"

"Gracias." Dije. Estaba un poco avergonzado.

Mi papá puso en marcha la camioneta y el hombre se alejó hacia quién sabe dónde, pero me di cuenta de que no iba a una casa. El hombre no tenía hogar, estaba seguro. Pero algo en él hizo que yo no quisiera dejarlo ir ... Lo miré con tristeza hasta que doblamos la esquina y luego, desapareció.

Las siguientes semanas, mientras andaba por el sendero en el bosque, pensaba cada vez menos en la casa del árbol y cada vez más en el hombre sin casa. Todos los días esperaba volver a verlo en el bosque, pero nunca lo vi. Choqué un par de veces, tratando de buscarlo, pero nunca lo encontré. Empecé a ir allí cada vez más, dos o tres veces al día, dejando de hacer cosas que normalmente hacia como ir a jugar con mis amigos.

No sabía por qué tenía tantas ganas de volver a verlo, pero era como una fuerza invisible que nos conectaba ... o algo cursi como eso ... no lo sé. La mayoría de los niños estarán contentos de tomar lo que sucedió como un buen recuerdo, pero yo no podía entenderlo.

Probablemente era solo curiosidad; Había leído libros sobre cosas como esta todo el tiempo. Y, además, también me disfrutaba de montar en mi bicicleta.

Pero como el tiempo no se detiene, y solo faltaba una semana para la carrera.

Fue entonces cuando me encontré con mis amigos. "Oye, Isaías."

"Oh hola-

"¿¡Dónde has estado!?"

"Por allí. Andando en mi bicicleta. Por el ...

"El sendero en el bosque, sí, lo sabemos. Vas allí todos los días, como tres veces. SIN PREGUNTARNOS NI NADA. ¡Ni siquiera nos has hablado en.... como una semana! Y la carrera no es sino hasta dos semanas todavía."

"Diez días." Aclaré yo

"No me salgas con tus cosas de nerd, hermano. Solo quiero que vuelvas a ser nuestro amigo." replico uno de mis amigos.

"¡Sí, soy tu amigo!" Reclame.

"Bueno, en realidad no. Los amigos hablan entre sí. Y tú....

"Quiero ganar la carrera, ¿de acuerdo?" - exclamé yo

"¡YO TAMBIÉN! Pero también quiero que todos seamos amigos y pasemos el rato y esas cosas." dijo otro.

"¡Podemos hacer eso luego de que gane la carrera!"

"¿Tu, ganar la carrera? Pregunto alguien-¡Pero si apenas acabas de aprender a montar!"

"Sí, pero como habrás notado, voy al sendero, ¡como 3 veces al día!"

"Eres tan gracioso." Respondió, pero note empezaba a enojarse.

"Lo siento, ¿de acuerdo? Pasaré más tiempo ustedes."

"Está bien, nosotros ... está bien...deberías..." Todavía parecía frustrado. "Mejor me voy"

Empecé a andar en bicicleta solo una vez al día y luego a tratar de pasar el rato con mis amigos, pero resulta que ellos nunca estaban en casa o no estaban disponibles, lo cual era bastante sospechoso. Me preocupé un poco por eso, pero traté de no pensar demasiado en eso.

Concéntrate en la carrera- me dije- Y eso es lo que traté de hacer, pero, con aquello que habían dicho mis amigos y el pensando en del hombre sin casa, simplemente no podía concentrarme.

Empecé a estrellarme cada vez más y empecé a llorar hasta quedarme dormido cada noche. Realmente me estaba estresando.

Unos días antes de la carrera, mi papá se dio cuenta. Había perdido el equilibrio por la ira y la frustración, y me caí al costado del camino. "Amigo, ¿qué te está pasando?" Preguntó mi papá.

Las lágrimas comenzaron a brotar de mis ojos.

"Yo ... no sé ..." y ahora sí que caían lagrimas a chorros por mi rostro y me sentí como un bebé sentado allí. Mi papá parado frente a mí me miraba con una expresión preocupada en su rostro, mientras yo pensaba en los amigos que estaban enojados y el hombre que nos ayudó... que no tenía casa...

Mi papá me llevó de regreso al auto, sin mi bicicleta, y me dejó en el auto solo, llorando, mientras él iba a buscar mi bicicleta al camino. Lloré y lloré hasta que olvidé por qué lloraba, y cuando al fin recordé y me di cuenta de que estaba llorando sin razón alguna.

Me calmé una vez que mi papá regresó a la vieja camioneta y cargó mi bicicleta en la parte de atrás. Me quedé dormido una vez que comenzamos a movernos.

Desperté en medio de la noche. Recordé lo que había sucedido y me sentí un poco avergonzado, pero estaba demasiado cansado para preocuparme tanto. Agradecí que mis padres me hubieran acostado y miré el reloj para ver qué hora era. Cinco en punto. Había dormido la mitad del día y toda la noche, y ahora aquí estaba. Pensé en lo que había sucedido el día anterior. Realmente necesitaba aplicar mi cabeza al juego.

Decidí leer para calmar mis pensamientos, pero solo ayudó un poco, porque mi mente quería seguir divagando.

Puaj.

Me levanté, me vestí, fui al baño y bajé las escaleras. Me senté en la cocina y apoyé la cara en la fría encimera, tratando de calmar mi mente acelerada. Eso ayudó un poco. Me quedé allí un rato, escuchando el zumbido del reloj y el frigorífico. El sol comenzó a salir lentamente cuando mi mamá bajó las escaleras.

"Buenos días." dijo, no respondí - "Papá me contó lo que ... pasó. ¿Estás bien?

¿Necesitas decirnos algo? " "No sé," murmuré.

"Cariño, no quiero que esto vuelva a suceder. Dime qué te molesta." "Supongo que solo estoy estresado".

"Entiendo," dijo. "¿Hay algo que podamos hacer para ayudar?" "Creo que solo necesito descansar".

"Sí." Respondió ella

Y eso fue lo que hice el resto del día y el día siguiente. Luego comencé a trabajar en mi bicicleta nuevamente y a concentrarme. Empecé a ganar velocidad y a mejorar en la forma de esquivar obstáculos, tanto mejoré que mi papa ya no podía seguirme.

Solo faltaban tres días para la carrera. Empezó a llegar gente de la península inferior, incluso de Detroit, Grand Rapids y Lansing. Incluso algunos niños vinieron del Canadá. El día antes de la carrera, mi papá y yo fuimos a inscribirnos. Vi a muchos niños, de 7 a 9 años, haciendo fila. Cuando llegamos al mostrador, la señora dijo que nos habíamos apuntado justo a tiempo y que solo quedaban unos pocos espacios. Me sorprendió bastante, ya que se suponía que había alrededor de doscientos cupos.

Apenas pude dormir esa noche. Me quedé dormido pensando en la casa del árbol que iba a construir y soñé con eso toda la noche.

Por fin llegó el día de la carrera. Estaba muy nervioso. Traté de componerme y sentirme feliz, ya que era esto por lo que había pasado semanas preparándome. Pero como ocurre en este tipo de cosas, no importa cuánto trate, continuaba estando nervioso ¿te imaginas? Hoy era el día.

Condujimos hasta el sendero, luchamos por encontrar un lugar para estacionar y nos dirigimos a la línea de salida. Encontramos nuestro lugar en el medio de la zona gruesa donde se aglomeraban participantes alineados y listos para la salida. La multitud era tan larga como una cancha de fútbol, y se extendía hacia atrás desde la línea de salida. Al menos eso era lo que yo sentía.

Bebí un poco de agua para detener la sensación de vértigo que tenía al mirar a los cientos de niños haciendo fila.

"Puedes hacer esto, amiguito. Recuerda concentrarte." me animaba mi papa.

"Sí." Contesté.

"Nos vemos en la meta."

"Nos vemos..."

Lo vi a un lado del camino mientras se unía a los otros padres, abuelos y seres queridos de todos los niños que se habían se alineado para la carrera. El árbitro o como sea que llamen a la persona que da el inicio a una carrera caminó hacia el costado de la línea de salida. La carrera estaba a punto de comenzar.

Puse mi pie en el pedal y el otro en el suelo para no caerme.

"¡En sus marcas!" preparo la bocina del arranque. "Prepárate ..." Vi a todos prepararse para partir, "¡y VAMOS!"

Todos volaron desde sus lugares de partida, algunos con inicios más rápidos que otros. Yo tuve un comienzo lento, y algunas personas me pasaron a toda velocidad, pero poco a poco comencé a ganar camino. Pasé por delante de dos personas y estabilicé mi paso junto a otras cuantas.

Me fascino observar todas las bicicletas. Rojo, verde, rojo y verde, blanco y negro y azul, y casi todas las combinaciones de colores que se te ocurran.

Empecé a tambalearme.

¡Pon atención! - me dije

Me estabilicé. Un par de personas me pasaron de lado y yo pasé a otras cuantas. Tenía que estar todavía en algún lugar entre el cincuenta o el cuarenta, pero todavía tenía tiempo para avanzar. Pedaleé más fuerte, pero iba prácticamente tan rápido como podía, pero solo pasé a un par de niños, y luego reduje la velocidad nuevamente. Traté de mantener el ritmo un poco más rápido y casi choco contra alguien.

"¡Oye, echa un vistazo a tu alrededor, hermano!"

"¡Perdón!" Grité, pero se fue a toda velocidad. Empecé a preocuparme.

¿Cuántas personas podrían alejarse así? ¿Cómo podría pasar a toda la gente que iba delante? ¡Había tantos!

No debo pensar así, me dije a mi mismo, y traté de observar cómo lo hacían los demás.

Entonces observe lo ellos hacían.

Todo lo que hicieron para acelerar fue pararse sobre sus pedales y caminar, como caminar sobre pedales. Lo intenté y casi me estrello contra alguien de nuevo.

"¡Oye, hermano, cuidado!" Puaj.

Lo intenté de nuevo, y esta vez fui capaz de estabilizarse y me dio control y velocidad. Pasé junto a algunos niños más y me volví a sentar. Estaba orgulloso de mi mismo. ¡Había aprendido algo!

¡Podría ganar!

Me había distraído de nuevo y casi chocó con otra persona. "¡Oye, cuidado!" En serio...

Me levanté de nuevo y pasé a otro niño. Necesitaba empezar a ganar más terreno.

Aceleré entre dos personas una al lado de la otra que parecían tener una conversación alegre, y que no parecían realmente estar compitiendo.

¡Alguien se había estrellado! Lo miré, pero no pude ayudar; Era mejor seguir y buscar ayuda cuando llegué a la línea de meta.

Habíamos llegado a la mitad de la carrera y el resto transcurrió sin incidentes. Acelerar, pasar gente, esquivar bicicletas y obstáculos físicos.

Pasé por delante de diez personas, pero todavía tenía de quince a veinte personas por delante. La gente comenzaba a aparecer al margen, gente animando a sus hijos y mirando.

¡UN MOMENTO!

Había alguien parado en medio de la multitud, sosteniendo un cartel de cartón que decía ¡¡PUEDES HACER ESTO!! Con letra desordenada. Lo reconocí de inmediato como el hombre sin casa. Cuando nos vimos, sonrió y él levantó su cartel y vitoreó.

Verlo finalmente después de tantas semanas, y AQUÍ, animándome, me llenó de energía como ninguna otra cosa podría haberlo hecho. Ya no quería ganar la carrera por el dinero, pero quería ganar por él.

Fui tan rápido que casi me caí directamente sobre el manillar. Pasé por lo menos a diez personas hasta que solo quedaron cinco o seis niños, algunos de ellos bastante por delante. No estaba seguro de poder alcanzarlos antes del final de la carrera. Pero tenía que hacerlo.

Me paré en la bicicleta para empujar a una persona más, a otra persona y a una más hasta que estábamos yo y otro niño delante de mí, y algunos que estaban demasiado adelante para ver. Traté de acelerar y esquive a la persona que estaba delante de mí antes, pero el mantuvo su ritmo.

¿Cómo iba a pasarlo? Traté de hacer lo del refuerzo de pie, pero él también lo hizo.

Cada vez más personas comenzaron a aparecer a los lados del camino. ¿Sería capaz de llegar en tercer lugar?

De repente, la persona a mi lado redujo la velocidad casi por completo hasta detenerse.

Miré por encima del hombro para ver qué había sucedido, pero había doblado una esquina y él se había ido.

Espero que este bien- pensé.

Pero ahora no era el momento de preocuparme; Necesitaba ganar esto. Aceleré un poco, pero los demás estaban fuera de la vista. ¿Estaba seguro de que había gente delante de mí, pero será que sí? La idea de estar en primer lugar me aceleró un poco. Solo pensaba en cosas buenas y motivadoras, con la esperanza de acelerar el ritmo a medida que el sendero se enderezaba en una pendiente larga y cuesta abajo.

Y allí, a cien metros por el sendero, estaba la línea de meta, con una persona cruzando y dos personas a punto de hacerlo.

Oh no.

Me disparé lo más rápido que pude, con la esperanza de alcanzar al menos a una de las personas que iban por adelante. Sin duda aquí fue donde fui más rápido de lo que había ido antes, y estaba ganando terreno rápidamente. ¡Los niños de adelante ni siquiera sabían que venía! ¡Todavía podría conseguir el segundo lugar!

Giré alrededor de una zanja hacia el lado izquierdo del sendero cuando pasé uno, y luego los dos niños de adelante. Deseé poder ver sus rostros atónitos mientras cruzaba la línea de meta.

La multitud aplaudió, algunas personas silbaron y oí sonar un cencerro. Mi papá y mi mamá corrieron hacia el sendero y me abrazaron y besaron y me levantaron en el aire.

"¡El segundo lugar son setenta y cinco dólares! ¡Estamos muy orgullosos, cariño! " "Has crecido mucho y has llegado tan rápido. ¿Qué diablos vas a hacer con tanto dinero? "

Me reía de emoción y felicidad, aunque no obtuve el primer lugar. El segundo lugar seguía siendo estupendo en contra de doscientos niños.

En cuanto al dinero ... Bueno, sé que tenía planes con él, pero ahora sé que alguien más lo merecía y necesitaba mucho más que yo. Tenía algo, o alguien más en mente.

About the Author

Elijah Kuiper is a 7th grader from Grand Rapids, who lives with his two brothers, parents, and his pet cockatiel, Chip. He has always loved reading and writing fictional stories, in English and Spanish. He's been creating art his whole life, drawing, playing piano and trumpet, and making stop-motion movies. He loves to learn about nature and animals, and sponsors the Cheetah Conservation Fund. He has taken Spanish Immersion classes since preschool.

Spanish Language Youth Judges' Choice Runner-Up

El Corazón Del Jaguar
Sophia Armas

En la profundidad de la Jungla Jenga, que significa venganza, se encuentra una tribu. Una tribu que protege el corazón del Guerrero Jaguar. Hubo allí una guerra en Jenga que nadie olvida. Jenga peleaba contra el dios Coyote. El dios Coyote mató a todos en su camino hasta que el Guerrero Jaguar llegó y usó su corazón para proteger a Jenga. Su corazón no permitía ni un dios bueno ni un dios malo pasar en las tierras de Jenga. Pero una diosa logró entrar. Y así comienza la leyenda.

Capítulo 1 Los gritos

Me levanté de prisa casi cayéndome de mi cama preocupada por no llegar tarde para el día de selección. ¡Escuchaba los gritos de la gente pidiendo ayuda "No te la lleves por favor! " . Cerré mis ojos. Respiré hondo. Me recordó el juramento de la reina Chiana. No hables en mi presencia al menos si te pregunto, no grites ni por alegría ni por tristeza, no te escapes de la tribu o los dioses te matarán y si haces algunas de esas cosas te expulsan por mi bien y el de todos.

Saqué mis nuevas botas del horno mientras admiraba el oro en ellas. Me las puse. No me quemaban por adentro, pero por afuera sí. Las botas estaban hechas para que si tu desobedeces te las quitan tus y las tiran para que se quemen y luego te expulsan. Abrí mi puerta al sentir la humedad y me dio un escalofrío mientras que vi la reina pasando con su ejército vestidos elegantes y ella en su carroza. Rápidamente me postré frente a mi casa para que no ser expulsada. Detrás de ella había 34 personas siendo jalados y latigados por los soldados. Entre ellos, distinguí a Ticki mi prima en la fila mientras la maltrataban y lastimaban con el látigo. Me miró y sonrió tristemente mientras la empujaban. En sus ojos podía ver esperanza y también tristeza. Sus ropas desgarradas y sucias con sangre y lodo.

Me levanté de donde estaba y corrí hacia ella. "No se la lleven!!!" grité mientras corría cerca de ella. Saqué mi espada que solo guardaba por si acaso. "Por Favor no se la lleven." Grité mientras que los guardias vinieron a atacarme. Vino el primer guardia. Me agache mientras que lo pateé en el estómago y mientras que se agrava el estómago por el dolor agarre una roca y le pegue en la cabeza. Nunca vi a los otros 4 delante de mí y detrás que me agarraron de los brazos. Me peleé con todos e intenté liberarme, pero los guardias me agarraban con fuerza. Ticki gritó e intentó librarse del lazo que amarraba sus muñecas.

Me libere y la abrace con fuerza. "Te amo mucho Tijax no me olvides. " Me dijo con suavidad. Luego me jalaron y me arrastraron lejos de ella. Grité y por primera vez dejé una lágrima caer. La lágrima que despertó al dios de tristeza. Ticki me gritó desde lejos y me dijo con voz ahogada" Te amo se fuerte! " y luego la llevaron a ser expulsada. La reina Chiana me ofreció a ver como la expulsaban. Le grité y le dije que no y que iba a pagar por lo que había hecho. Los guardias me amarraron a un poste y me dejaron allí por la noche. "Tijax?" dijo una voz tranquila. ¿Estás muerta? Pregunto preocupado. Me reí "No le preguntes a un muerto si está muerto" contesté, con una risita. No podía ver a la persona que me hablaba y ya no lo escuchaba. ¿Hola? ¿estás allí? no había sino silencio. Miré al cielo y me pregunté, ¿porque el dios del dolor hace esto? De repente, unos ojos amarillos me miraban desde el otro lado del escudo. Los miré y vi una sonrisa con dientes que brillaban. Grité, pero ya no estaba allí cuando parpadeé. Rápidamente me intenté liberar, pero no podía. Desde lejos podía escuchar la ejecución y los gritos de dolor y tristeza. Entonces sentí el espíritu de Ticki ser libre. Ya no sentía dolor y ya no respiraba en este mundo.

La sentí hablar dentro de mí. Ahora me tocaba a mi cargar el peso de la nueva generación, pero me pedía tener precaución porque la reina no era una buena persona. " ¿Por qué tengo que preocuparme de ella? " pregunté, pero la voz en mi mente ya no estaba. Después de unas horas me quedé dormida en un sueño que jamás olvidaré. Era todo lo que ocurrió cuando falleció Ticki. Sentí que me arrastraban y desperté para ver que los guardias me llevaban al palacio.

Capítulo 2 La Reina Chiana

Abrieron las puertas de jade y oro. Al final del largo pasillo se sentaba la reina Chiana. Estaba acariciando su leopardo.

¿Porque mataste a Ticki? ella era leal a ti! Me miró con un poco de tristeza." Mi niña, solo lo hice porque ella levantó una revolución en contra de mí." Me dijo con firmeza. "Llévenla a la selección y que quede indefensa, déjenla pelear hasta morir. "Me llevaron y me pusieron en una carroza llevándome a la selección. Me bajaron y vi que había cientos de personas listas para verme morir oh mejor dicho...verme vivir. Los guardias me lanzaron en el centro del coliseo. "Señoras y señores hoy vemos a una desgraciada morir contra el puma endemoniado!! La reina se levantó de su trono admirando la gente que le aplaudía con fuerza. Había una gran jaula siendo cubierta con una gran manta. Las señoras enfermeras estaban aplicándole pociones de rabia al gran gato. "Listo, peleen. Grito con emoción. Se levantó la manta y se abrió la jaula y salió el gran puma. Sus colmillos más grandes que una lanza, sus ojos rojos como un fuego ardiente, sus grandes garras como 3 veces más grandes que un machete y 3 veces más filosas, y por fin su pelaje negro como la oscuridad con sus manchas grises. Me di cuenta de que en la oscuridad alguien me sonrió, y esa era la misma sonrisa que había visto en la oscuridad, pero los ojos no eran los mismos. SLASH!! Sin que me diera cuenta el puma me había rasguñado con sus garras horriblemente filosas. El color rojo se esparcía rápidamente desde mi mano herida y en la boca del puma pude ver uno de mis ojos que él había arrancado. Rugió y de repente escuche una voz familiar que decía "De prisa levántala y llévatela yo montaré al puma y tu Shira lanza tu lanza hacia la reina para que se concentren en ella y su herida y no en nosotros. dijo con voz de líder. Ayuda por favor.' Pero solo vi oscuridad.

Capítulo 3 El secreto

"Ven aquí Tijax te voy a contar algo" era la voz de Ticki- ¿Que paso Ticki? Dije con preocupación. Splash!! Me levanté de mi sueño y sentí agua fría sobre mi rostro, y un dolor tremendo en el ojo derecho. Me lo toque y había un parche. Mire a mi alrededor. Estaba sentada en una cama y había medicina en una mesita. Parecía como un templo debajo de la tierra. "Buenos días Capitana Tijax está lista para la guerra?" me habló la voz familiar. "No la presiones Tarm sabes que no sabe nada todavía". Dijo una voz seca y fría. "Hola soy Chepita y bienvenida al cuartel que Ticki construyó y organizó." Dijo Chepita.

" ¿Que es todo esto, y donde estoy" grite con temor " ¿Por qué Ticki hizo esto y nunca me lo dijo?, ¿porque tengo un parche?, ¿porque...?"

"Por favor deja de hablar, despertarás a Dacrón y te van a regañar por hablar más que su abuelita." Dijo Tarm Tranquilo.

"La reina es la diosa de la que todos hablaban, quien entró por el escudo y busca obtener el corazón del Jaguar." Por cierto, me llamo Shira." dijo fría y seca.

"¿Por qué lo quiere? ¿Por qué quiere el escudo? " Pregunté casi ahogando mi voz.

"Lo quiere porque el Corazón del dios Jaguar es muy poderoso y destruiría el escudo que protege a Jenga. Shira me respondió.

"Fíjate que lo tenemos en este templo subterráneo porque Ticki lo encontró cuando estaba excavando oro para la reina y ahora nosotros lo protegemos. Porque no vas al almacén de armaduras para buscar la tuya, tendrás que pelear, todos vamos a pelear." Chepita me miró con sus ojos profundos como el mar. Me levanté de la cama para caminar por el pasillo. La verdad no sabía a donde iba, pero me había propuesto ir a explorar.

Capítulo 4 El ataque.

Concluí que el pasillo era interminable y entonces decidí entrar en la biblioteca para preguntar dónde estaba el almacén de armadura. Entré y había millones de libreros llenos de libros. Seguí caminando y admirando los libros. Me tope con una gran caja de vidrio puro y adentro estaba el corazón expuesto en toda su hermosura. ¿Porque lo guardarían en una biblioteca?! ¡Qué tontería! Toqué el vidrio y de repente vi que el corazón estaba a metros bajo la tierra y solo había una ilusión que lo hacía aparecer como si estuviera flotando en el medio de la biblioteca. Pero no era sabio anunciar que estaba aquí, en medio de la biblioteca para que todos vieran su... ¡¡BOOM!! Todo el templo tembló con fuerza y brusquedad. Escuchaba el ejército de adentro del templo marchar justo sobre. Salí corriendo de la biblioteca. ¡Ayuda!dijo una señora atrapada debajo de unos escudos. Rápidamente corrí hacia ella y la levante todos los escudos hechos de jade fino y verde. De Repente sentí una fuerza tremenda y los levanté de un tiro a todos los escudos. Sentí que mi pupila se pasó de ser redonda a ser una línea recta" Gracias." me dijo. No le respondí porque se acercaba algo grande y horrible. Tenía cientos de pies que parecían palos, pero hasta el final tenía algo con filo. Gruñí y el monstruo largo y asqueroso rugió como el infierno. Saltó en el aire y rasguñe lo que parecía unos de sus cientos de ojos. Rugió con rabia y le salió sangre morada. De Repente se me salieron las garras. Estaba lista para darle otro golpe, pero me di cuenta de que detrás de él estaba Shira, Chepita,Tarm y otro que asumí era Dacrón. Chepita era chiquita y tenía los oídos puntiagudos. Tarm era serio con ojos rojos y piel oscura. Shira era alta, seria, y los ojos verdes, Dacrón estaba encapuchado no sabía quién era. Tarm salto y pateó al monstruo en la cara y Shira le disparó con su arco. "Vamos sígueme" dijo Chepita, con voz aguda quien ya estaba en frente de mí. Empecé a correr, pero ella me llevaba ventaja. De repente sentí que corría sin esfuerzo y la alcance sin problema. "Izquierda y hacia arriba de las gradas después, abre las puertas y Tarm te esperara afuera!" ¿Como? -pensé. Pero cuando antes de poder contestar ya estaba peleando con el monstruo. Empecé a correr otra vez recordando me cuando Ticki me cuidaba. Había alguien que la cuido a ella cuando sus padres fueron a la selección. Ella me llevaba 13 años. Ya había llegado a la puerta. La abrí y vi una gran batalla entre monstruos peleando: leones, y el gran puma endemoniado me sonrió mientras atacaba a los guardias de la reina.

Capítulo 5 El poder.

Estaba lista para morir por algo que no sabía que existía, algo que mi prima había hecho para proteger una cosa que salvaría a Jenga. Saqué mis garras y empecé a buscar a Tarm. Vino mi primer oponente era un monstro gordo, me pego duro y volé para luego golpearme en contra de una roca que me saco el aire. Me levante adolorida. Se venía hacia mí, esta vez con un mazo. Salté sobre él y aterricé detrás de él, clavándole mis garras en su cabeza. De Repente sin darme cuenta agarré una mano que intento tirarme una lanza. Le di un puño en el estómago y lo lancé hacia otros monstros gordos que corrían hacia mí. Salte alto en el aire examinado el espacio antes de caer. Salté otra vez con fuerza y examinado el área con cuidado. De Repente vi a Tarm y la Reina peleando. Rápidamente dirigí mi caída allí y le pegué con mi puño a la reina. Ella cayó al piso y se levantó quitándose el maquillaje lo que la hacía parecer una persona imperfecta. Se levanto rugiendo. Tenía la cara de un coyote, pero el cuerpo de una persona. ¡Lo siento! " le grite a Tarm " Pero que hiciste la convertiste y la enojaste y veo que descubriste que cuando el puma te rasguño te dio pode...." De Repente ambos nos vimos volando. Tarm chocó en contra de unos soldados de la reina. Yo pude rebotar de el árbol a darle un golpe a la reina. Cayó, pero yo no fui la suficiente rápida para ver la patada que venía hacia mi cara. Me pego y luego usó su fuerza de coyote y fue tan duro que no pude ver ni oír nada más. Me dolía el ojo derecho y me dolía la cabeza.

Capítulo 6 El golpe final.

"Levántate rápido." me dijo Tarm dándome unas cachetadas. Me levanté adolorida viendo que mi parche no estaba en mi ojo derecho si no en el piso destrozado.   Me levanté y Tarm apuntó a las puertas para ir al templo subterráneo. Asumí que la reina había huido hacia allá porque no la veía en ningún lugar. Rápidamente le dije que viniera, pero dijo que me ganaría tiempo antes de que marcharan los soldados de la reina al templo. Le dije que gracias, pero había cientos de soldados ya adentro. SLASHER!! grito Tarm. de repente vino el puma endemoniado y me hizo una seña Tarm para que me subiera. "No! ni en tus sueños... esa cosa casi me mata y.." antes de terminar de hablar el me interrumpió diciendo: "Pero estas aquí en persona y viva. Ahora súbete o todo Jenga morirá. Lo mire callada. Me subí y volamos saltando sobre cada persona y todos los soldados. Al fin, aterrizamos en la biblioteca. Salté y vi a la Reina pegándole al vidrio. Me abalancé en actitud de ataque, pero en vez de eso quebré el vidrio.

"¡Niña tonta el poder es mío!" Gritó la reina con su cara de coyote. Pero cuando lo agarró, el corazón del Jaguar explotó, haciendo explotar también a la Reina. Chepita vino corriendo. "Pero qué paso?". Dijo con voz aguda. "Ticki jamás escondió el corazón aquí, sino que lo escondió en algún otro lugar secreto, seguramente muy lejos de acá." Respondí yo.

Apunte al polvo del corazón que explotó y esta había formado palabras que lo explicaban todo. Reparamos el templo y yo fui coronada como la nueva reina. La ciudad está libre de las reglas horribles de la antigua reina y todos vivimos bien. Bueno, eventualmente tenemos algunas dificultades con los dioses, pero eso es todo.

El Fin.

About the Author

Sofia Armas is 12 years old. She was born in Guatemala City and was raised by her Guatemalan father and US-born mother. Sofia was homeschooled until moving to Michigan. She has always loved creating stories and making them come alive. Sofia's writing is influenced by her Guatemalan roots and the legends of the Mayan stories she learned from her father and grandparents.

Spanish Language Youth Readers' Choice Winner
El Indiano
Miguel Rafah Reagan

¿Quieres que te cuente una historia?

Busca una silla y siéntate, que te la voy a contar, pero quiero que sepas que esto no es invento, es la historia de nuestros antepasados, y es real.

Muchos años antes, tantos que ni se pueden contar, en la montaña sagrada, nació un niño indígena, el Indiano al que le gustaba subirse a los árboles y pasaba horas jugando a brincar de un árbol a otro; cuando le daba hambre su alimento eran las frutas. Le gustaba la guayaba, el mango, el guineo maduro, la guanábana, el zapote y todas esas frutas de colores contentos y alegres; las olía porque sus olores le agradaban y se las comía con gusto. Comía muchas, ni llevaba la cuenta, Las iba probando y comiendo. Cuando terminaba una fruta botaba las semillas a la tierra, ni cuenta se daba de lo que hacía hasta que miró detrás de él y vio que de esas semillas que había botado nacieron más árboles y de esos árboles muchas más frutas salieron, y por donde el había andado jugando, comiendo frutas y tirando las pepas se había convertido en algo hermoso, muy verde con mucha naturaleza. Muchos árboles, muchas flores y muchas frutas. Había tanta fruta, que llegaron muchos animales a vivir ahí. Por eso a ese niño le llamaban Colibrí. La montaña sagrada estaba tan feliz con Colibrí por haberla ayudado que decidió regalarle unos dones y uno de esos dones era el don de hablar con los animales. Otro don era que podía hablar muchos idiomas diferentes.

Fue así como Colibrí se hizo amigo de todos los animales, pero sus mejores amigos eran Kunsamunu el cóndor, que era muy sabio, volaba muy alto y lo veía todo, hasta a la hormiguita más chiquita. Trataba siempre de ser justo con todos los habitantes de su casa, la montaña sagrada.

El otro mejor amigo de Colibrí era Tanika una Jaguar, que siempre decía la verdad y solo comía mangos, sus favoritos eran los mangos verdes con limón y sal. Tanika siempre estaba con Avena, el ave del paraíso. Se llevaban todos muy bien, Avena con su pico le bajaba los mangos más verdes a Tanika y era muy generosa siempre dándole muchos mangos verdes. Avena era muy buena, le gustaba cantar y vivir en armonía con los demás, hasta con el conejito Tewe, aunque Tewe conejo era muy tramposo e hizo una trampa para atrapar a Tanika. Tanika decía siempre la verdad y también le gustaban las frutas, por eso no se enteró de que en una de ellas había una trampa! Pero allí estaba Colibrí mirando y gritó "¡Oye Tanika , cuidado! ¡El conejito te puso una trampa!" Tanika lo escuchó y busco otro lugar para seguir comiéndose las frutas.

En la montaña hay una regla: los animales no pueden salir del hábitat por su seguridad. ¡Pero claro, un día Tewe se salió! Y este bandido Tewe no era un bebé sino un adulto. Ya una vez afuera tuvo que salir corriendo y se esconderse porque unos hombres que cortaban árboles para construir casas lo vieron y lo querían cazar para comérselo. Lo persiguieron hasta la montaña sagrada y al ver esos árboles grandes pensaron en cuanta madera hermosa podían sacar de ellos y cuánto dinero ganarían al venderla. Pero Kunsamunu , el cóndor, los vio desde lejos y le contó a Colibrí lo que pasaba. Colibrí empezó a mecerse de árbol en árbol y finalmente tiró unas frutas que les pegaron a los tres hombres blancos Pam! Pam! Pam! Y gritó en su mejor inglés posible "Hey! Stop that, or I'll hurt you!" pero ellos no le hicieron caso y él tuvo que volver a usar otras frutas con las que les pegó otra vez a los tres blancos Pam! Pam! Pam! Y estos se huyeron corriendo ¡pero mientras lo hacían, cayeron en la trampa de Tewe!

Colibrí les preguntó a los blancos "What are you doing?"

"We want to make a house." dijeron. Y le explicaron que ellos cortaban árboles para construir sus casas, y que estaban cortando árboles cuando vieron un conejo y lo quisieron cazar para comérselo. Que lo siguieron y descubrieron esos árboles tan grandes.

Kunsamunu le dijo a Colibrí, ellos no deben cortar nuestros hogares, en estos árboles viven muchos animales, las aves, hacen sus nidos en las ramas, en los troncos hacen nidos las ardillas, hasta en las raíces viven las hormigas!

"Es verdad", dijo Tanika.

Avena como era generosa y le gustaba la armonía, le dijo a Colibrí que si ellos lo que querían era madera para construir, que ella les enseñaría los árboles que estaban caídos, secos y muertos para aprendieran a usar esos y a no cortar los árboles de la montaña.

Colibrí les señaló:

"Take that tree! It fell after a storm and now is dead"

"Ok." Dijeron los blancos y los hombres indígenas los ayudaron a cargar los árboles secos hasta donde ellos vivían.

Los animales estaban tan felices, que celebraron con Colibrí y sus amigos, ¡y hasta invitaron a Tewe a la celebración!

¡Es así como Colibrí, junto con sus amigos, protegieron por siempre a la montaña sagrada!

About the Author

Miguel Rafah Reagan was born in Grand Rapids, MI. His mother, a Colombian immigrant, taught him Spanish. At age 2, Miguel was reading in both English and Spanish. His favorite subjects in school are Math, Language, Science, Art, and Spanish. In his free time, he loves playing with friends, soccer, Legos, and playing Vallenato and Cumbia, the traditional Colombian music on his accordion. He loves writing poems, short stories and reading. Miguel visited Colombia when he was little, but he hopes he can go back soon to visit La Sierra Nevada in Santa Marta, the place that inspired him to write the story El Indiano.

Spanish Language Youth Published Finalist

El poder de la amistad

Sylvia Fisher

¿Por qué tengo que dibujar? ¡Estoy aburrida! Mi maestra de arte, Sra. Woodland estaba enseñándonos cómo dibujar personas de forma realista. Mi dibujo se ve como si hubiese sido aplastado por un coche, atacado por lobos salvajes, y como si se hubiera golpeado la cabeza un millón de veces.

Arte es una clase electiva. Escogí arte solo porque a mi mejor y única amiga, Emmy le gusta. Yo no necesito más amigas. ¡Emmy es la mejor de todas las amigas!

—Esta vez pueden escoger a sus parejas de trabajo —dijo Sra. Woodland— Dibujen el rostro de ellos realísticamente como les enseñé.

Yo corrí hacia Emmy.

—¡Hola, Emmy! —grité—. ¡Vamos a sentarnos allí en las sillas que dan vueltas! Esas sillas son el lugar dónde Emmy y yo siempre nos sentamos.

—Lo siento, Amy —contestó Emmy—. Ya hice pareja con Zoe.

—Oh. Ok. —dije tristemente. Emmy siempre es mi pareja.

—No estes triste. Podemos ser pareja mañana. —dijo Emmy tratando de hacerme sentir mejor.

Suspiré. La Sra. Woodland casi nunca nos deja escoger a nuestras parejas.

—Está bien. —dije—. No siempre necesitamos ser pareja.

No tengo otras amigas en esta clase. ¡No tengo otras amigas en toda la escuela! La última persona que queda es, ¡Joe Smith! ¡El niño más extraño de toda la escuela! Él es un cerdo. De verdad. No te imaginas ni quieres saber lo que está debajo de su mesa. Hay cientos de envoltorios de dulces que él no debería tener en clase. Chicle medio masticado está atorado en la parte de abajo de su mesa. También escribe cosas raras en su escritorio como, Esta escuela es *mala, quiero irme a casa, o ¡Navidad!*

-Dibuja tu primero —dijo Joe—. Pero dibuja mi cara así. Y hace una mueca sacando la lengua

—No pienso que la Sra. Woodland quiere que dibujemos eso —dije.

—Aguafiestas —respondió Joe, pero puso su cara normal otra vez.

Era muy difícil dibujar su cara porque él no se quedaba quieto y siguió hablando con su amigo Henry. Estaba yo en medio del dibujo cuando sonó la campana.

—¡Libertad! —gritó Joe.

Él y sus amigos salieron del salón corriendo.

—¡Escuchen! ¡Chicos! Regresen al salón y vuelvan a salir otra vez en orden —gritó Sra. Woodland. Esto es algo que todas las maestras hacen cuando las personas corren en los pasillos.

Cuando un maestro dice esto, todos pensamos que es un maestro malo.

Me sentí muy bien cuando salí de la escuela y casi quise gritar como Joe.

Arte es mi última clase. Hoy es viernes, ¡el mejor día de toda la semana! Emmy vive en el mismo vecindario, entonces cada noche del viernes voy a la casa de Emmy para dormir o ella viene a la mía. ¡Es la cosa más divertida en todo el mundo! voy a preguntarle en cuál casa vamos a dormir. La alcanzo a ver. Esta caminando con una niña popular, Zoe.

—¡Hola, Emmy! —dije—. Quería saber en cuál casa vamos a dormir hoy.

—Pues… —Emmy pensó—. Hoy voy a dormir en la casa de Zoe.

—¡Sí! ¡Ya planeamos todo! —dijo Zoe con entusiasmo—. Vamos a construir una fortaleza con almohadas, comeremos helado con caramelo caliente, veremos una película de monstruos ¡y hacer pulseras de amistad!

—¡A mí me encantan todas estas cosas! —respondí—. ¿Puedo venir?

Sería tan bueno dormir en la casa de una niña popular. Si duermo allí, esto significa que yo también soy popular porque Zoe *solo* juega con otras niñas populares. Me emociona imaginar esto. Pero Zoe contesto:

—Sera la próxima vez, Amy. Esta vez es solo para nosotras.

—Sí. La semana que viene podemos dormir juntas ¡Te prometo! —dijo Emmy.

—Pero… ¿Por qué no puedo venir esta vez? —pregunté tristemente—. Yo soy muy divertida cuando me conoces. ¿Verdad Emmy?

—Sí, eres muy divertí…

—Pero yo no quiero bebés durmiendo en mi casa —interrumpió Zoe.

—¡Zoe! —gritó Emmy—. ¿Por qué dijiste…

—Porque es la verdad —interrumpió Zoé otra vez.

—¡Yo no soy un bebé! —grité—. ¡Y mejor que no voy a ir, porque yo no quiero dormir con una niña mal educada!

—Pues mejor así para todos —dijo Zoe poniéndose la mano en la cadera. Emmy miró hacia abajo, pero continúo caminando con Zoe.

Nunca le he caído bien a Zoe. Ella no es muy amable y siempre está diciendo cosas que no son verdad sobre personas que no son populares. Personas como yo. ¡Una vez Zoe anuncio a todos en la escuela que yo me hacía pipí en la cama!

¡No me he hecho pipí en mi cama desde que tenía cinco años! También dijo que todas mis calificaciones son una D. ¡Y la verdad es que yo solo saco A y B! Zoe es la niña más popular en toda la escuela. *Todos* saben su nombre y ella *solo* juega con otras niñas populares.

¿Esto significa que mi mejor amiga es una niña popular? ¿O solo significa que a Zoe ella le cae bien?

Esa noche no quería hacer nada aparte de estar con Emmy. Normalmente a esa hora, Emmy y yo estaríamos comiendo chocolate juntas en su cama y compartiendo nuestros secretos. Pero en vez de eso, estoy llorando sobre mi almohada. Esa noche debería haber sido divertida pero no lo fue.

El lunes después de la escuela, escuché que Zoe y Emmy estaban hablando de su tiempo juntas. Noté que el borde de su pelo estaba teñido de morado oscuro. Y el pelo de Zoe estaba teñido de rojo.

—¡Hola Amy! ¿Te gusta nuestro pelo? —preguntó Emmy mostrándome su pelo morado.

—Sí. Es muy bonito —respondí.

—El teñido fue un regalo por mi cumpleaños —dijo Zoe.

—Tomó mucho tiempo, pero valió la pena —dijo Emmy.

—¡Y no dormimos sino como a la 1:30am! —dijo Zoe.

—¡Y comimos tanto helado! —exclamó Emmy.

—Suena muy divertido —dije.

—¡Tan divertido que vamos a hacerlo otra vez la próxima semana! —dijo Emmy.

—¿Qué? —grité enojada—. ¡Tú me prometiste que ibas a dormir conmigo!

—Oh...Olvídate de esto —Emmy miró a Zoe. —Lo siento, Zoe. Pero Amy tiene razón. El viernes yo le prometí eso.

—Supongo que está bien... —dijo Zoe.

Aunque Zoe dijo que estaba bien, su cara la delataba con la verdad. Parecía que quería matarme.

—Pero —dijo Zoe firmemente—. Si vas a dormir en la casa de Amy esta semana, necesitas prometerme que vas a dormir en mi casa la semana que viene.

¡No voy a dejar que Zoe robé a *mi* mejor amiga! - pensé yo.

—¡Y luego conmigo la semana siguiente! —grité.

—¡No! —gritó Zoe—. ¡Yo merezco tener dos semanas seguidas porque tú duermes con ella cada semana!

Sus ojos parecían llamas de fuego.

—¡Pues tu no mereces dormir con *mi* amiga ni una sola vez! —grité—. ¡Emmy era *mi* mejor amiga antes de que tú te la robaras!

—¡Yo no me la robé! ¡Ella *quiere* ser mi amiga! ¡Probablemente más que contigo! ¡Porque ella quiere siempre hace pareja conmigo y no contigo!

—¡Esto no es verdad! —discutí.

—¡Paren de gritar! —gritó Emmy.

Pude ver lágrimas en sus ojos. Por un momento todas nos quedamos calladas. Era un silencio muy tenso. Tanto así que se podían oír los pájaros cantando y por un momento yo quise ser uno de ellos, con una vida mucho más sencilla que la mía.

—Vamos, Emmy —dijo Zoe rompiendo el silencio. Luego me miró, y dijo— yo y Emmy vamos a hacer nuestra tarea juntas hoy.

Sentí como si iba a vomitar. *Realmente se está robando a Emmy.*

—¿Te veo mañana? —preguntó Emmy tímidamente.

—Solo si quieres malgastar tu tiempo conmigo —le dije.

Emmy miró hacia abajo y empiezo a caminar con Zoe. No me gustó como la tomo de la mano.

—¡Espera, Emmy! —grité— ¡Olvidé decirte algo!

—¿Qué? —preguntó Emmy.

—Tengo una competición de baloncesto. Vas a ir ¿verdad?

—¡Por supuesto! ¡Siempre voy a tus juegos! —dijo Emmy alegremente.

—Es este sábado —le dije.

—Entonces, ella no puede ir —dijo Zoe.

—¿Y por qué no? —le pregunté con mis manos en la cadera.

—Emmy ya me prometió que iba a ir a mi competición de gimnasia —dijo Zoe.

—Pues… necesito pensar. No sabía que Amy también tenía algo el sábado —contestó Emmy.

—Pues ella va a ir conmigo porque ella siempre va a mis juegos —dije—. Y, ¿por querría ella ir a una competición de gimnasia? Eso es aburrido y estúpido.

—¡No más estúpido que el baloncesto! —exclamó Zoe—. Eso es para niños.

—¡No lo es!

—¡Sí!

—¡No!

—¡Sí!

—¡Yo soy muy buena en baloncesto! —le grité en su cara.

—¡Y yo estoy en el nivel más alto en la gimnasia! - respondió ella.

—¡A cuál vas a venir! —ambas cuestionamos a Emmy en unísono.

Cuando dejamos de gritarnos, nos dimos cuenta de que Emmy ya no estaba allí.

—¡Probablemente está llorando! —grité. —¡Esto es todo por tu culpa!

—¡Si tu no hubieses hablado sobre tu estúpido baloncesto, esto no habría pasado! —gritó Zoe.

—¡Pues es tú culpa porque tú te robaste a *mi* amiga!

—Como ya dije, ¡yo no me la robé! A Emmy le gusta más estar conmigo así que seguro va a venir a mi competición. ¡Lo cual no tiene nada de estúpido!

Y con esta nota, Zoe se marchó dejándome otra vez en el silencio.

Emmy va a venir a mi competencia, ¿verdad? Yo soy su mejor amiga, ¿verdad?

Ese sábado, estaba muy nerviosa. Yo soy buena en baloncesto, pero no *tan* buena. Mi entrenadora, la Sra. Payton estaba hablándonos sobre nuestras estrategias para ganar.

—¡Escuchen, chicas! —gritó la Sra. Payton—. El equipo al que enfrentamos es muy bueno. Pero no vamos a dejar que ellas nos ganen, ¿verdad?

—¡No! —todos gritamos—. ¡Vamos a ganar!

—¡Esta es la actitud que quiero!

Cuando salimos a la pista de baloncesto, yo miré alrededor y busqué a Emmy.

Seguramente está en algún lado. Seguro ella no quiso ir a una competición de gimnasia.

No tuve mucho tiempo para buscarla porque el entrenador del otro equipo sonó la campana para empezar el juego.

¡La Sra. Payton no estaba exagerando cuando dijo que el otro equipo era bueno! Ellas agarraron la pelota al principio y se quedaron con ella la mayoría del juego. Comparadas a ellas, nuestro equipo es malo. Muy malo.

El puntaje final es 8 a 2. Ellas ganaron. Cuando por fin metí la pelota en el aro, no oí gritos de Emmy como normalmente ella lo hacía. Y cuando salí del edificio, Emmy no estaba allí esperándome con flores amarillas.

—¡No lo puedo creer! —me quejé con mi mamá cuando entré a la casa—. ¡No es justo!

—Tal vez Emmy quiso ir a la competición de Zoe —sugirió mi mamá—. Emmy no es solamente tu amiga. Ella tiene la libertad de tener otras amigas aparte de ti.

—Pero yo soy su mejor amiga —dije, aunque ya no sabía si eso era verdad—. Ella siempre va a mis juegos, ¡pero hoy ella no estaba allí! -reclamé.

—Lo siento, Amy —dijo mi mamá—. Pero es bueno tener más amigas aparte de Emmy.

—Nadie más quiere ser amiga mía —me quejé.

—¿Has tratado de hacer amigos?

—Pues... No —contesté—. Pero es solo porque nunca había necesitado más amigas. ¡Yo tenía a Emmy!

—Pues estoy segura de que Emmy todavía quiere ser tu amiga —dijo mi mamá.

—Si ella de verdad quisiera, hubiera venido a mi competición y no a la de Zoe.

—Tal vez es hora de tratar de hacer más amigos —sugirió mi mamá.

Al próximo día en escuela, vi a Emmy otra vez caminando con Zoe. ¡Ella ni me saludo! Pasé muchos días sentada sola en almuerzo porque Emmy se sentaba con las niñas populares. Yo no soy suficientemente popular para sentarme con ellas. Además, cada viernes Emmy iba a la casa de Zoe para dormir en vez de venir a la mía. Un lunes, no quise ir a escuela. Me hice la enferma, pero mi mamá, que tiene superpoderes, sabía que no era verdad, así que tuve que ir a regañadientes.

En mi primera hora, había una estudiante nueva.

—Quiero que todos saluden a Lola —anunció mi maestra—. Ella se acaba de mudar de California.

Lola saludó con su mano y le sonrió a la clase. Tenía frenos de arcoíris y dos colas de caballo. Quería decirle hola, pero ella tenía su asiento en el otro lado de la clase.

Lola no estaba en ninguna de mis otras clases antes del almuerzo, así que, como todos los otros días, me senté sola. Realmente quería sentarme con Lola. Pensé que tal vez si realmente trato, podríamos ser amigas. Pero no hice ni dije nada. No sabía qué decir.

En el autobús al fin del día, Emmy está sentada con Zoe y las otras niñas populares y no conmigo. Decidí tomar el consejo de mi mamá y realmente tratar de hacer más amigas.

Caminé hacia ellas.

—Hola. ¿De qué están hablando? —pregunté sentándome con otra niña.

—Estamos hablando sobre esta niña nueva, Lola —dijo una niña, señalando a Lola quien se sentaba sola en el frente del autobús.

—Quería hablarle en el almuerzo, pero...

—¿Han visto como se viste? —me interrumpió otra niña.

—¡Sí! —dijo Emmy—. Parece a una niña de preescolar.

—¡Realmente! —dijo Zoe riéndose—. ¡Sus colas de caballo son ridículas!

—¿Cuántos años tiene? ¿Tres? —dijo la niña con quien me había sentado.

—Y ¿Quién le pone a su hija el nombre de Lola? ¡Ese es un nombre estúpido!

Pues a mí me gusta su nombre - respondí yo

—¿En serio, Amy? —me pregunto Emmy.

Al menos me está hablando- pensé yo.

—Sí. Lo he visto —dije.

—¿Has visto sus frenos? ¡Ella los tiene en orden de arcoíris!

—No lo he notado —dije mirando hacia abajo.

¿Por qué estas niñas están hablando así de Lola? Solo porque ella no se ve

bien no significa que no sea amable.

Realmente quería moverme de asiento, pero el autobús había comenzado a moverse y no quería meterme en líos.

Las niñas siguieron hablando así el resto del viaje. Yo pensaba que sus frenos eran bonitos y que su pelo era lindo también. Quería decir algo, pero si lo hacía, las niñas dirían cosas así sobre mí también. Yo sé que no soy una persona popular. Al menos esto es lo que Zoe piensa, y si Zoe piensa así, todos los demás pensarán lo mismo.

Al día siguiente durante el almuerzo vi a Lola otra vez sentada sola. Quería sentarme con ella mucho más que antes y decidí ser valiente.

—Hola... ¿Tu nombre es Lola, ¿verdad? —le pregunté tímidamente.

—Sí —respondió ella. Sus ojos azules se encontraron con los míos.

—Hum... ¿Está bien si me siento aquí? —pregunté.

Lola sonrío tan ampliamente que pensé que su cara iba a explotar.

—¡Eso me encantaría!

Tomó apenas dos días para que Lola y yo fuéramos amigas inseparables. ¡Ella es igualita a mí! Odia la clase de arte y le encantan las matemáticas y ciencias. Siento como si un ladrillo pesado hubiese sido levantado de mis hombros. ¡Mi mamá estaba en lo correcto! Solo necesitaba tratar de hacer más amigas. La semana siguiente será mejor...

—Hola, Amy —dijo Emmy casi susurrando—. ¿Por favor, podemos ser amigas otra vez? ¡La vida no es lo mismo sin ti!

No estaba lista para perdonarle.

—Ni siquiera me hablabas —dije cruzando mis brazos—. ¿Por qué?

—¡Porque quería ser popular como Zoe! Ella me dijo que si quería ser popular no podía hablar con alguien que no sea popular. Dijo que eres un bebé y que los bebés no son populares entonces que no podía hablarte. ¡Pero tú eres la persona más popular que conozco! —Parecía que Emmy estaba a punto de llorar si no la perdonaba.

—¡Está bien, Emmy! ¡La vida tampoco era lo mismo sin ti! —dije aliviada de que a Emmy aun le caía bien.

Nos abrazamos por un tiempo muy largo. Podía oler su champú de fresas y kiwi.

—Hola —exclamo Lola caminando hacia nosotras—. Tu debes ser Emmy. ¡Amy siempre está hablando sobre ti!

—Sí, soy Emmy. —dijo.

—Emmy, quiero que conozcas a mi amiga, Lola —dije yo.

Rápidamente Emmy y Lola se convirtieron en amigas. Emmy confesó que ella había hablado mal sobre Lola, pero dijo que eso no era lo que ella realmente pensaba.

Esa semana todas dormimos en la casa de Lola. ¡Lola tenía cuatro perros y tres gatos!

¡Eran adorables!

Nos reímos y hablamos durante casi toda la noche. Hicimos postres de helado con caramelo caliente, crema batida y por supuesto, muchas grageas de arcoíris.

—¡Este es cien veces mejor que el que me comí con Zoe! ¡Porque ahora estoy comiendo con mis mejores amigas! —exclamó Emmy abrazándonos.

About the Author

Sylvia is a 7th grader who lives in Grand Rapids with her family, which includes two supportive parents, a younger sister, younger twin brothers, and two bunnies. Sylvia loves ballet and performs with Creative Arts Repertoire Ensemble. Sylvia is a native English speaker but has been learning Spanish in a Spanish immersion program. She loves to read and write, and usually writes stories in English, but decided to write a story in Spanish for this contest. After entering short stories for several years, Sylvia's thrilled to finally have a story published! Her dream job is to become an author.

Spanish Language Youth Published Finalist

Por el amor de la música
Liliana Orange

"¡Mami por favor no!" Yo grité. Mi mami no entiende, ella quiere que yo tenga un buen descanso esta noche, pero, yo quiero ir a pedir dulces esta noche en Truco-o-Trato.

"Ay, Gabriella, no. Si vas a pedir dulce, no vas a tener un buen día de los muertos."-protestó ella.

"¡Pero no quiero ir!" grite yo. Corrí a mi cuarto y empecé a llorar. No quería revivir los momentos que tuve con Papi. Mi papi era el mejor, me enseñó como manejar una bicicleta, cómo caminar y hasta cómo hablar. Pero también me introdujo a la música. Él me entendía. Cuando yo escuché la primera canción fue la cosa más maravillosa que he oído en mi vida. Y ni siquiera tenía letra, solo eran los instrumentos tocando una melodía maravillosa. Después de esto escuchaba canciones todos los días. Pero ahora, nunca las oigo. Papi está muerto y no puedo hacer nada por eso. Seguía llorando cuando Mami vino a mi cuarto.

"Ay, mi amor, no sabía qué ir a pedir dulces en Truco-o-Trato significaba tanto para ti."

Yo no dije nada, la cosa no es que Truco-o-Trato signifiqué mucho para mí. Es que Papi no está aquí, y sin el no quiero celebrar el día de los Muertos. Si Papi estuviera aquí nunca pensaría en ir a Truco-o-Trato, pero porque él no está, y ni siquiera quiero pensar en tener un día de Muertos sin él.

"Por favor, mi amor, dime lo que pasa." dijo Mami. Pero no puedo, ella no lo entendería. Es como si ni siquiera supiéramos que Papi no está. Mami sabe que él está muerto, pero ella no entiende que yo no quiero pensar en él.

"Mami, tu no entiendes, por favor déjame en paz y déjame ir al Truco-o-Trato." dije yo. "Ay, si eso es lo que quieres, pero quiero que estés en casa a las 10, no más tarde." respondió ella.

"Ok" respondí con alegría. Pero en realidad, todavía no estaba alegre. Solo quiero a papi conmigo. Si su malvado trabajo no le hubiera pedido ir a recoger algo de la oficina esa noche, él todavía estaría aquí conmigo y con nuestra familia. Lo que pasó fue que la oficina de mi padre que se llama CDs de Oaxaca, lo llamó por teléfono. Le dijeron que querían que él viniera a la oficina a recoger un nuevo CD que debía escuchar. Era muy urgente, así que él fue a la oficina muy tarde por la noche. Luego de recoger el CD y mientras manejaba de regreso a casa por la autovía, alguien chocó la parte trasera de su carro. El carro tambaleó descontroladamente afuera de la autovía, y quedó muy mal. La policía y también la ambulancia llegaron hasta allí. Mami y yo estuvimos en el hospital visitando a papi todos los días después del choque. Pero cada día su salud iba de mal en peor. Fueron 5 días después del choque que papi murió. Antes de que el muriera me dijo esto:

"Mi maravillosa Gabriella quiero que sepas cuanto te amo. Quiero que tu protejas a tu mamá y a tu hermana, si yo no estoy."

Yo estaba triste y sorprendida porque ese día fue cuando me enteré de que iba a tener una hermana y que quizá mañana papi no estaría. Esa noche yo lloré mucho. Y como era de esperar papi se fue. Así que deje de escuchar canciones desde ese día. Hace ya un mes. Ahora necesito cuidar a mi mamá, pero también a mi hermanita. Mi hermanita María es una gran responsabilidad. Ella necesita mucho cuidado, pero está bien porque la amo.

Agarré mis cosas para ir a Truco-o-Trato.

"Mami ya me voy, vengo a las 10." Dije.

"Ok" contestó mami. entrando la habitación con una toalla en sus manos. "Te amo Gabriella, sé muy cuidadosa"

"Ok" le prometí. Salí de la casa, y mi primer año de ir Truco-o-Trato empezó. Pensé que cuando salga de casa hoy, todas mis preocupaciones desaparecerían.

Cuando entré a la casa todas las cosas del Dia de los Muertos estaban preparadas. No había siquiera pensado en esto mientras estaba en Truco-o-Trato. Mami me recibió con María durmiendo en sus brazos.

"¿Cómo te fue?" preguntó con voz baja. "Bien" respondí.

"Ay que bien" dijo. "¿Estás lista para celebrar el día de los muertos?"

preguntó.

¿Cómo responderle a eso? Debo decir la verdad o diré solo que estoy cansada. "Estoy muy cansada" mentí

"Mija, creí que ibas a ir Truco-o-Trato y luego venias aquí, lista para el día de los muertos." "Lo siento Mami, pero no me siento muy bien y estoy cansada" mentí aún más. Pero en realidad no me sentía bien, era ese sentimiento de extrañar.

"Son todos eses dulces" dijo ella mientras tomaba mi temperatura con la mano.

"Ay, mami estoy bien solo muy cansada, no me siento lista para celebrar el día de los Muertos ahora." le dije.

"Por favor Gabriella, hazlo por papi" rogó. Yo corrí a mi habitación y me metí en mi cama. Como dije antes, mami no me entiende, ella no entiende. ¿Por qué ella no es tan triste como yo, aun cuando ella estaba enamorada de papi? No tiene sentido. Oigo a mamá venir a mi cuarto. No trae a María.

"Puse a María a dormir. Gabriella por favor dime lo que pasa, quiero ayudarte." me dijo.

Solo quiero a papi. ¿Le digo a ella o no? Mi corazón dice que sí, pero mi mente dice que no. ¿Qué debo decir? ¿A quién debo seguir? ¿A mi mente o a mi corazón? Haré lo que me dicta la mente, ósea mi cabeza, literalmente.

"Mami es que este fue mi primer año de Truco-o-Trato y la cabeza me duele por todo el ruido, Solo necesito dormir, quizá mañana estaré lista para el Dia de Muertos." le dije.

"Ok" dijo mami, "Que tengas un buen sueño" se despidió.

Cerré mis ojos y tuve un sueño. Hay un tocadiscos, y están dando vuelta, una y otra vez sin parar. No es un buen sueño. Quizá es una pesadilla, pero recuerdo a papi. Me hace sentir mareada, quiero llorar y vomitar a la vez. Creo que sí es una pesadilla. Cuando me levanto, mamá tiene decoraciones por todas partes para el día de los muertos, y música. Ahora si tengo ganas de vomitar. Corrí hacia mi cuarto, llorando. Otra vez mami me preguntó, si estaba bien, y me dijo que ella quería ayudar y otras cosas. Esta vez le hice caso a mi corazón.

Le dije esto:

"No mami, extraño a papi muchísimo. No quiero celebrar el día de los Muertos sin él, así que trate de irme a Truco-o-Trato para no tener que celebrarlo. Lo siento"

"Ay mijita, no necesitas mentir, te amo y estoy aquí por ti y para ti. Te entiendo. Estamos en esto juntas." me dijo que realmente tenía la determinación de hacer lo que estaba diciendo que haría.

1 mes después

"Si mami" le contesté. Desde esa mañana mami realmente hizo lo que dijo. Cuando me veía triste o yo no era la misma, mami se sentaba y a hablar conmigo. Yo me estoy recuperando rápido con la ayuda de mami. Y creo que estamos más cerca, la una de la otra, mucho más que nunca antes.

Un día mami puso una canción que a mí me gustaba antes que papi no estuviera. ¿Cómo pudo hacer eso?, todavía me dolía. Pero aun así seguíamos siendo muy cercanas. Tomamos turnos cuidando a María y también cocinando la cena.

Un día María enfermó muy seriamente y necesitaba ir al hospital. Mami estaba tan preocupada que ni siquiera quería dejar el hospital. Yo dormía por la noche sin mami algunas veces. Era muy serio. Cuando Mami regresó al hospital me pidió ir al ático para buscar unos papeles médicos. Los doctores creían que María tenía neumonía. Yo estaba muy nerviosa y emocionada porque nunca había ido al ático así que no sabía qué pensar. Estaba lista para la aventura. Ni siquiera sabía dónde era la entrada para subir al ático. Resulta que está en el techo del armario dentro de la habitación de mi mamá. Había escaleras muy chirriantes. Subí hasta ver el ático oscuro. Había tanto polvo, cajas de ropa vieja, papeles y otras cosas, pero también un gran baúl. Tenía curiosidad de ver lo que estaba en ese baúl, pero sabía que mami estaba impaciente y tenía prisa, así que busqué la caja que decía Archivos Médicos. Después de encontrar esto busque un archivo llamado María Juana Lopez. Encontrar el archivo tomó tanto tiempo, que mami me pidió que me apurara dos veces. Finalmente, lo encontré y bajando las escaleras, y se lo dí a mami.

"Qué bueno, que lo encontraste. Espero que este archivo sea la respuesta. Esta es la última vez que voy a pasar la noche en el hospital. No quiero que tu estes aislada. Te quiero Gabriella." Diciendo esto, se fue al hospital. Aunque debería estar triste de ver a mi mamá irse, era más mi curiosidad de ver lo que había en el gran baúl. Corrí al cuarto de mami y abrí su armario para ver el techo donde estaba el ático. Vi una cuerda colgando del techo. Yo brinque para tratar de agarrarlo, pero todavía era demasiado corta. Corrí de la habitación para encontrar algo en lo que me pudiera parar. Finalmente encontré una caja de madera que era suficientemente fuerte para sostenerme.

Lo agarré y lo llevé al armario de mami. Lo puse en el suelo y me subí en él, después de dos o tres intentos finalmente logré agarrarlo y lo jalé hacia el suelo. Al instante las escaleras se vinieron al suelo. Me subí y corrí al baúl, primero lo admiré por afuera. El baúl era de color verde con un poco de turquesa. Era hermoso. Cuando lo intenté abrir estaba cerrado con llave. ¡No puedo abrirlo! No sé dónde está la llave. Estaba tan emocionada, pero ahora estoy triste. No sé dónde está la llave. No tengo ni idea. Estoy aún más triste porque podrían ser años hasta que encuentre la llave. Podía agarrar un martillo y empezar a destrozarlo. Pero el baúl es tan precioso y hermoso que no puedo. Bueno no puedo abrir el baúl. Bajé las escaleras y escondí la caja de madera en su ropa. Cuando mamá regresé yo no ví a María esto significa que ella todavía no está bien.

Quiero preguntar sobre ella, pero estoy muy impaciente para tener las respuestas del baúl. Me acerqué a ella y pregunté:

"Mami cuando estaba buscando los archivos vi un baúl grande que es un color verde y también un poco de turquesa. Cuando saliste fui otra vez al ático y traté de abrirlo para ver lo que era, pero está cerrado con llave. ¿Sabes dónde está la llave?"

"Ay Gabriella ya no sé." contestó ella.

"¿Qué quiere decir esto?" pregunté.

"Bueno, es que tu papi me dijo donde estaba la llave para dártela ti en tu cumpleaños. Él me lo dijo antes de morir, pero ahora no sé dónde está." explicó. Esto no puede estar pasando. Ahora estoy triplemente triste porque, primero, no puedo abrir el baúl. Segundo, quizá nunca pueda abrir el baúl. Y tercero, porque era un regalo para mí de parte de papi.

"Gracias por contarme esto mami," Ahora si le pregunté sobre María, "¿Cómo está María?" "Bueno creen que ella tiene neumonía, pero no entendí el resto de lo que me explicó.

"Gracias mamá, es bueno saber, como puedo ayudar? dije.

"La cosa es Gabriella que no sabemos cuándo ella va a salir del hospital" explicó

"Oh, bueno espero que ella esté bien y salga del hospital pronto."

Fui a mi cuarto y lloré. Mami me ayudó mucho a no llorar y quedarme calmada. Pero ahora estoy llorando. Lloro porque nunca voy a tener chance de abrir mi regalo del baúl de papi, y no sé si María está bien. Y más que nada quiero que todo sea como antes.

Papi debería estar aquí, María debería estar aquí con nosotros y no en el hospital, ni enferma. Solo quiero que todo sea como antes, más que nada quiero que todo vuelva a ser normal.

Me desperté y algo muy incómodo estaba bajo mi almohada. Veo una caja azul pequeña, la abro y encuentro una llave. ¡Mami la encontró! Estoy tan emocionada de ir y abrir el baúl. Con la llave también veo una carta. Lo abrí y al instante sé que es una carta de papi por su letra. Dice esto:

¡Feliz Cumpleaños Gabriella! Espero que estés bien. Mami probablemente te dio este regalito. Siento mucho no estar allí, pero te amo muchísimo. Te di esta llave porque hay un baúl en el ático que quiero que abras. Te quiero mucho, espero que recibas este regalo y abras el baúl.

Te amo, tú papi.

Trato de no llorar, pero las lágrimas solo vienen y no pueden parar. Aunque estoy triste estoy emocionada también porque ¡ahora tengo la llave! ¡Y puedo abrir el baúl!

Voy a la cocina donde encuentro a mami llorando mientras cocina. Me siento mal por ella. Fui y le di un abrazo con fuerza.

"¿Ay Gabriella cómo estás?" ella pregunta

"Bien mami, pero ¿por qué lloras?" le pregunté.

"Bueno, María está en el hospital por 5 días, no sé si está bien. Esto es muy estresante. No quiero que te estreses." dijo. No sé qué decir "Veo que tienes el regalo"

"Si, lo encontré debajo de mi almohada, gracias mami" "De nada. Pasé toda la noche buscándolo hasta encontrarlo" dijo mami. "Gracias mami por todo" contesté.

"De nada, y no te preocupes ¿quieres desayuno?" preguntó.

"Quizá más tarde! Ahora quiero abrir el baúl" le dije a mami con ansiedad. Caminé hacia su cuarto y fui a su armario. Agarré la caja de madera y deslicé la caja a la entrada del ático. Agarré la cuerda y las escaleras salieron al suelo. Las subí y corrí al baúl. Le admiré por fuera, agarré la llave y lo abrí. Lo que veo es magnífico. Veo discos de diferentes artistas y canciones. Al fondo veo un tocadiscos de color amarillo, mi color favorito.

"Mami ven acá" ella viene corriendo al armario. "Qué pasa?" ella dice subiendo las escaleras. "Mira esto" dije mostrándole a ella el baúl.

"Wow es bonita" dijo.

"Yo sé, pero mira adentro" sugerí. Ella miró y puso una expresión de WOW en su cara. "Mira todo esto, es magnífico" dijo.

"¿Podemos ponerlo en mi cuarto? quiero oír la música." pregunté.

"¿En serio mija?" de acuerdo. "Ok podemos, pero debemos empezar ahora." Logramos bajar las escaleras, y en la cocina tomamos un descanso, cuando el teléfono sonó. Mami contestó. Hubo un silencio y después ella dijo.

"Eso es magnífico gracias doctor" y colgó. "¿Que es magnífico?" pregunté.

"Tu hermana está bien solo era una fiebre, vuelve a casa mañana." contestó con alegría. Esto está bien.

"Estoy tan agradecida" dije.

"Yo también" dijo mami, "debemos terminar de mover este baúl antes que María venga"

Cuando finalmente lo pusimos en mi cuarto, agarré el tocadiscos y lo encendí. Ahora miré en el baúl y traté de escoger una canción. Hay muchísimas, pero no pude escoger. Al fondo veo un disco con una nota que dice:

Gabriella esta es una nota de papi. Este disco era el que fue a buscar urgentemente. Nunca lo escuché, pero quiero que tú lo oigas conmigo. Te quiero, papi.

Puse el disco en el tocadiscos. Empezó a tocar. La música instrumental era magnífica. Pero las letras eran aún más especiales. Iba así:

Mi amor, mi amor más lindo, te quiero.

Eres la música a las letras y el sol, las nubes. Linda, linda que eres mi amorcito.

Te quiero más y más.

Y aunque no estoy ahí contigo. Mi amor nunca se va a terminar.

Eres la cosa que quiero aún más y más. Pero no llores, no llores mi amor.

Te quiero, te quiero más y más.

Cuando el sol desaparece tu sonrisa es mi sol. Tu sonrisa es el sol. Te quiero mi amor.

Empiezo llorando de tristeza, pero también de felicidad. Felicidad porque María está bien, mami está bien y aunque papi no está, él todavía me quiere. Empecé el disco de nuevo porque no había oído una canción en meses. Y nunca había oído una canción tan bella en mi vida.

Un año después.

"¡Gabriella! ¿Dónde está María?" preguntó mami.

"Aquí conmigo" contesté. Ahora que María tiene un año y le estoy enseñando la canción de papi. Desde la primera vez que la oí, la llamé "Te quiero".

Mami vino a mi cuarto y vio a María sentada en mi regazo y a mi sentada en el suelo.

"Ha! ahora estás enseñando esta canción a María" ella dice.

"Si" digo, "ahora que ella tiene un ano pensé que podría ensenarle la canción a ella" "Bueno si es una canción muy bella." mami dice. María empieza a rizar. Creo que a ella le gustaba la canción.

"Yo le voy a dar a María algo de comer." mami dice y recoge a María. Ella sale del cuarto. Desde que papá murió yo aprendí una lección. La lección es que, aunque las personas no están ahí contigo no significa que no puedes ser feliz. Ellos viven en tu corazón y en canciones, poemas y más. Debemos enfocarnos en lo que pasa ahora pero también debemos recordar los momentos buenos, en vez de los malos. Pero más que todo, las personas deben de ser recordadas. De cualquier manera, que lo hagas, hay que recordarlos. Y compartir esto con todo el mundo para que ellos también lo oigan.

El fin.

About the Author

Liliana Orange is a 12-year-old from Jenison, MI. She enjoys expressing herself through writing and acting, often writing scripts. She also enjoys playing violin, soccer and volleyball. Liliana has a passion for traveling with her family and spending time in nature.

Spanish Language Youth Published Finalist

¿Dónde está mi casa?
Sophia Toboy

Un día la Tortuga Gula estaba muy preocupada porque no podía encontrar su casa. Caminó por las calles y el parque de su ciudad, pero no podía encontrarla.

Entonces le preguntó a Ratón Ratoni: "Ratoni, ¿me ayudas a buscar mi casa?"

"Sí, claro" le contestó y ambos comenzaron a buscar la casa de Gula por toda la ciudad: la escuela, la heladería favorita de Gula, la tienda de quesos de la mamá de Ratoni, pero nada de nada.

Cuando ya estaban muy cansados se encontraron con Lolo, el sapo.

"Lolo, he perdido mi casa" dijo Gula muy triste, "¿nos ayudas a encontrarla?"

Lolo, miró a Gula y con una sonrisa muy grande dijo, "Gula, tú llevas tu casa encima", "¿Acaso se te olvido buscarla allí?"

Gula, Ratoni y Lolo rieron por horas porque no podían creer que se les olvidó buscar la casa en el lugar más fácil y Gula se alegró muchísimo de tener un amigo tan servicial como Ratoni y un amigo tan inteligente como Lolo.

About the Author

Sofia Joy Toboy is a first grader in an Spanish Immersion program in Grand Rapids, MI. She loves speaking Spanish and spends most of her summers in Spain, where she has family and friends. Sofia loves reading, playing with her dolls, exercising outside, and writing. Her favorite topic to write about is animals. She has written more than 10 short stories and in all of them there is at least one frog, her favorite animal. When she grows up she wants to be a veterinarian or a zookeeper.

About Write Michigan

The Write Michigan Short Story Contest began in 2012 as a dream. Kent District Library Director Lance Werner envisioned libraries and publishers working together to highlight the efforts of Michigan writers via an independently published book. What better way to interest readers and writers than a writing contest? Writers could create a short story; readers could read those short stories. Nearly 600 writers from all over the state entered the inaugural contest. Author Wade Rouse contributed the foreword to the first anthology.

For the tenth annual contest, founding partners KDL and Schuler Books and new partners Canton Public Library, Traverse Area District Library and Hancock School Public Library received submissions from 264 zip codes across the state of Michigan, including the Upper Peninsula. With almost 1,200 entries, the contest had 131 reviewers to narrow the field to ten semi-finalists in each category. Ten judges, including some of last year's winners, determined the Judges' Choice and Runner-Up winners with almost 2,400 public votes cast to determine the Readers' Choice winners in each category. Cash prizes amounting to $5,000 were distributed to the winners.

With such overwhelming success, the Write Michigan Contest has established itself as a premier writing contest in the Mitten State. Libraries and bookstores share the goal of fueling interest in libraries, writing and reading. The Write Michigan Short Story Contest is an integral part of that goal.

2022 Judges

Adult Category

BONI ASHBURN

Boni is the author of eight picture books for children, including *I Had a Favorite Dress* and *The Class*. She manages the Hancock School Public Library in the Upper Peninsula, where she lives and reads and writes. She has four grown children (who still manage to keep her quite busy) and one cute dog. You can learn more about Boni at www.boniashburn.com.

LISA MCNEILLEY, PHD

Lisa is a writer and educator. She taught writing at the college level for over 15 years before starting Writer's Alley, LLC. She wrote *Need to Know College Success,* which was awarded grants from the Wege Foundation and Michigan College Access Network. She is co-author of *D.B. Cooper and Me* and her poetry has appeared in Ariel Chart. Lisa started the Cascade Writers' Group and serves as facilitator. Lisa served as editor of Imagine *This! An ArtPrize® Anthology* and was prose editor for *The 3288 Review.*

LIENE STRAUTNIEKS

Liene is a Learning and Development Specialist in HR at Spectrum Health. She is an avid supporter of the arts and has been a volunteer in the Grand Rapids theatre community for the past 15 years. She wrote her first short story, "Dahlia," for the Write Michigan 2020 competition and won runner-up in the adult category. Liene is very proud to now be a published writer and is looking forward to publishing more work in the future. She lives in Grand Rapids with her wife.

Teen Category

ABIGAIL KLOHA

Abigail is a senior at St. Johns High School who loves reading, writing, learning languages and playing the piano. She plans to attend college to major in creative writing and/or Spanish.

DEBI MARKEE

A lifelong reader and writer who is passionate about children's literature, Debi holds an MFA in Writing for Children and Young Adults from Vermont College of Fine Arts. Working with children for more than 30 years, Debi reads across genres and writes the same way. She currently works part-time as a substitute teacher and a writer.

MELISSA MILLER

Melissa graduated from Taylor University with a Bachelor's Degree in English Education. She received a Master's Degree in Linguistics from Cornerstone University. Melissa spent the first nine years of her career as a middle school English and ESL (English as a Second Language) teacher. She currently works part-time as a Children's Program Director for Ada Bible Church. Melissa and her husband, Nate, reside in Middleville and have two boys ages 8 and 4. In her spare time, she enjoys organizing, reading, painting her nails and shopping.

Youth

KAREN MCPHEE

Karen fell in love with writing when her fourth-grade teacher taught her how to diagram sentences while encouraging her to think of words as paint on canvas. Her career included six years as a television news journalist and 35 years in education, during which time she served as a communications director, superintendent, education policy director and strategic planning consultant. Now retired, she lives in West Michigan with her husband Marty and enjoys traveling, hiking and photography. She's two thirds of the way through writing her first novel, which she hopes to finish sometime this decade.

JOSH MOSEY

Josh is a veteran bookseller turned published author who now works for Kent District Library. Books are kind of his thing. His recent publications include *Man of Purpose, The Case for Christ Devotions for Kids* (with Lee Strobel) and *How to Fight Racism Young Reader's Edition: A Guide to Standing Up for Racial Justice* (with Jemar Tisby). For a semi-complete list of publications, visit joshmosey.wordpress.com.

Spanish-Language Youth

RUBÉN CAMPOS

For over 28 years Rubén has worked in the book world, including Studium (his bookstore), Grupo Planeta (his first publisher), Mr. Books (the best bookstore chain in Ecuador) and Kent District Library (his first library job). Rubén considers himself to be blessed to have two citizenships (Ecuadorian and US). He is an avid reader, librarian and book lover who believes in the power of changing the world to make it better where he has control, by eating sustainable and supporting local businesses. Rubén also is an advocate for the power of libraries to make our communities better and stronger.

RAMÓN PERALTA

Ramón is from the Dominican Republic and has been living in Grand Rapids since 1982. His education: Bachelor's degree in Philosophy and History (University of Santo Domingo), a Master's degree in History (Michigan State University). He is the coauthor of two books: *Azucar, Encomiendas y otros Ensayos Históricos* (1979) and *Religión, Filosofía y Política en Fernando A. de Meriño, 1857-1906* (1979). He was a professor of Dominican History in the University of Santo Domingo. In Grand Rapids, he worked for 26 years in Grand Rapids Public School in Adult Education and as a Family Support Specialist at the main office of GRPS. He has been a columnist for 28 years in "El Vocero Hispano," a Hispanic newspaper in Grand Rapids. He is currently enjoying retirement.

Acknowledgments

For the past ten years, the Write Michigan Short Story Competition has helped authors share their stories with the world. This has been made possible, first and foremost, by authors of all ages who put pen and pixels to paper to tell stories of love, life, adventure, pain, healing and more. This year, nearly 1,200 entries were received from across Michigan, vying for a chance to be featured in this anthology. We applaud each one for sharing.

More than 130 volunteers reviewed the entries this year, not only scoring the entries but also providing each author with helpful feedback. The review process determined finalists which were advanced to a panel of judges who, like the authors, are deeply passionate about writing. We are profoundly grateful for the judges: Boni Ashburn, Lisa McNeilley, Liene Strautnieks, Abigail Kloha, Debi Markee, Melissa Miller, Karen McPhee, Josh Mosley, Rubén Campos and Ramón Peralta.

We are also deeply grateful for Stephen Mack Jones for providing the foreward to this anthology and delivering the keynote address at the Write Michigan Short Story Awards Ceremony.

The generous support and partnership of Schuler Books, Canton Public Library, Hancock School Public Library, Kent District Library and Traverse Area District Library has been exceptionally valuable in reaching out and inviting authors from across the state to participate in this year's contest.

Thanks also to the Write Michigan Committee for tirelessly organizing, promoting and bringing fun to the short story contest: Brad Baker, Diane Cutler, Randy Goble, Janice Greer, Kip Odell, Sara Proano, David Specht, Remington Steed and Katie Zuidema.

Lance Werner, Executive Director of Kent District Library, and Bill and Cecile Fehsenfeld, owners of Schuler Books, have been steadfast champions of this project since day one.

Our appreciation goes to Artist Adolfo Valle for providing us with the beautiful Write Michigan artwork. You can see more of his work at adolfovallestudios.com.

Ultimately, thanks go to you, our readers, for reading and voting on finalists, telling others about the contest, visiting libraries around the state and encouraging writers to put their words on paper to share the power of expression through short stories.

Diane Cutler, Kent District Library
Pierre Camy, Schuler Books

Sponsors

SCHULER BOOKS

Chapbook Press

meijer

Canton Public Library

HANCOCK SCHOOL
PUBLIC LIBRARY

Schuler Books
Self-Publishing Services

Thanks to Schuler Books' Espresso Book Machine, we can help you print your book. You provide us with two PDF files (one for the cover and one for the text or bookblock) and we will print a high-quality paperback book for you, in color or black and white. The Espresso Book Machine can print books from 40 pages to 650 pages long.

What are the benefits of printing your work with Schuler Books?

- This is your book.
- You'll receive one-on-one support
- Since you sign a non-exclusive contract with us, you may pursue any other publishing venture that you choose.
- You retain all rights to the printed work, and you have complete control over layout, content and design.
- No minimums. You may print one copy or as many as you want.
- You retain rights for non-exclusive distribution and may sell books printed at Schuler Books or with the Chapbook Press through any avenue.
- Modifications are allowed at any time, for an additional fee.
- You set the book price and determine the royalty per book.

What we need to print your book

2 print-ready PDF files: one for the book and one for the cover, formatted the way you want them to look. We will upload your files and print a paperback edition of your book on high quality (archival) paper and a full-color glossy cover, in any size you want from 5"x 5" to around 8" x 10.5"

We can help you get there

We can help as much or as little as needed in each area of making your book a reality.

New Services:

- e-Book /Global distribution print and digital package: Your title (in print or as an eBook) will be available for purchase to over 39,000 global retailers, and their customers. The eBook will be available for more than 70 different Ereaders including Amazon Kindle, Apple iBookstore, Barnes&Noble NOOK, Kobo, Sony, etc.) Bookstores and retailers around the world will be able to order your book for their customers.
- Title set-up:
  - Book and e-book: $520 (includes 2 ISBNs)
  - Book only: $420 (include 1 ISBN)

You need to order a minimum of 50 copies within 60 days of title set-up.

Additional orders (minimum quantity of 10), require a three week notice.

- Epub Conversion: $0.80 per page (page count is based on the total number of pages in your bookblock)
  - Conversion will take three weeks.
  - For Printing costs and author compensation please ask for a quote.

Chapbook Press

Chapbook Press

	Short Run	Standard Package	Chapbook Press Publishing
	$50 Plus Production Costs	**$150** Plus Production Costs	**$300** Plus Production Costs
Maximum Print Run	20 Copies	Unlimited	Unlimited
Page Maximum	100 Pages	650 Pages	650 Pages
Personal Consultation	30 Minutes	30 Minutes	60 Minutes
Email Support	Limited Support	Included	Included
PDF Review	No	No	Yes
Proof Copy	1 Proof Copy	1 Proof Copy	1 Proof Copy
PDF Upload	Includes initial upload No Re-uploads	Includes initial upload +1 Re-upload	Includes initial upload +1 Re-upload
Cover	Basic Text Cover	Basic Template Cover	Basic Template Cover
Saved for Re-prints	No	Yes	Yes
ISBN/Barcode	No	No	Yes
Library of Congress Reg.	No	No	Yes
Books in Print Reg.	No	No	Yes
Sale: Schuler Books	No	No	Yes
Sale: SchulerBooks.com	No	No	Yes
Production Costs	$7.00 per copy flat rate	$6.00 per copy +$0.03 per page	$6.00 per copy +$0.03 per page
Color Interior	No	+$0.15 per page	+$0.15 per page

A la Carte Sevices	Freelance Fees
PDF alterations (re-uploads): $25 (+ price of proof copy)	Pre-press file consulting: $15 per 1/4 hour
Scanning: $50 deposit / $50 per hour	Manuscript evaluation: $250
File conversion to PDF: $5	Manuscript editing: $135 deposit, $45 per hour
Cover from template: $50 (prepay)	Proofreading: $105 deposit, $35 per hour
ISBN & barcode acquisition: $100	Transcribing: $105 deposit, $35 per hour
Amazon listing: $50	Coaching: $50 deposit, $50 per hour
Library of Congress Registration: $50	Custom cover design: $100 deposit, $50 per hour
Additional consultation time: $40 per hour	Page layout: $100 deposit, $50 per hour
Additional PDF adjustments: $60 per hour	Hardcover Binding: Ask for a quote.

For more information visit SchulerBooks.com

Want to talk to someone? Call us today at 616-942-7330 x558,
or email us at: printondemand@schulerbooks.com

www.ingramcontent.com/pod-product-compliance
Lightning Source LLC
Chambersburg PA
CBHW071935190726
48293CB00004B/1263